Inside the Eurovision Song Contest

About the Author

Julian Vignoles was born in 1953. After qualifying from UCD in 1976, he worked at *Hot Press*. He joined RTÉ in 1979 and worked in radio and television for many years, in several roles. He took charge of Ireland's Eurovision entries on seven occasions. Between 2006 and 2011 he was an elected member of the governing body of the Contest, the Reference Group. He is the author of *A Delicate Wildness: The Life and Loves of David Thomson 1914-1988*, published by Lilliput Press in 2014.

INSIDE THE EUROVISION SONG CONTEST

Music, Glamour and Myth

Julian Vignoles

Photos by Kyran O'Brien

To Deidne,
For great Eurovision
times together!

Best wishes

The Liffey Press

Julian

Published by
The Liffey Press Ltd
Raheny Shopping Centre, Second Floor
Raheny, Dublin 5, Ireland
www.theliffeypress.com

A catalogue record of this book is
available from the British Library.

ISBN 978-1-908308-71-9

Printed in Spain by GraphyCems

Contents

Acknowledgements

As Irish Head of Delegation for seven Contests, I shared highs and lows and interesting times with a group of Irish artists who represented their country with courage and determination at Eurovision: Jedward, Brian Kennedy, Niamh Kavanagh, Chris Doran, Sinéad Mulvey and Black Daisy, Donna and Joe McCaul, Dustin and Dervish. And there were backing singers, among them Nikki Kavanagh and Leanne Moore, and other team members like Terry Heron, Stuart O'Connor and Peter Canning.

I met some great people in my years as a member of the Reference Group, and they were generous to me with their advice and recollections: Svante Stockselius, Stina Greaker, Federico Llano, Kjell Eckholm, Kati Varblane, Diana Mnatsakanyan, Jonatan Gardarsson, Jan Frifelt and Jill Paulsson.

My RTÉ press office colleagues were great when we got into scrapes, at home and abroad: Sharon Brady, Tara O'Brien, Rayna Connery and Dymphna Clerkin. I also shared Eurovision camaraderie with colleagues Kevin Linehan, Deirdre Horlacher, Gráinne Ní Fhiannachta, Marty Whelan, Larry Gogan, Derek Mooney, Bridgette Horan, and Paul G. Sheridan. I have quoted from several writers on Eurovision and I'm grateful to them: John Kennedy O'Connor, Adrian Kavanagh, Tim Moore, and Karen Fricker and Milija Gluhovic. I thank Francis Duggan for his verse about Noel C. Duggan. There are several

Irish journalists who brought informed coverage of Eurovision over the years, among them Ken Sweeney, John Waters and Eddie Rowley.

Helpful analysis and advice during the work came from Carol Louthe, and my sons, Rory and Eoghan. My friend Tim Lehane cast a meticulous eye on the manuscript. Diarmuid Furlong, Seán Farrell and Aileen Dillane were also supportive. Wikipedia's reproduction in great detail of Eurovision voting results was a valuable research tool. Paddy O'Doherty gave me great help with my draft manuscript. Diane Barker and Aoife Maher proofread.

A key element of this book comes from the eye of Kyran O'Brien, with whom I shared adventures over several Eurovision assignments. I'm pleased that his photographs are published here. All pictures are by him, unless otherwise credited, those in Chapter 9, or those from the work of Albin Olsson. Sietse Bakker of the EBU gave permission to use photos on Eurovision.tv by Andres Putting.

I'm delighted Larry Gogan agreed to write the Foreword. Crucially, David Givens of The Liffey Press enthusiastically published this book.

Foreword

I'm a Eurovision fan. It's extravagant. It's fun. And the music can be really good too.

The first time I went to the Eurovision Song Contest was in 1978, when Tom McGrath, the RTÉ producer of the Irish end of the show, asked me to go to Paris to do the television commentary. I had never done a TV commentary before and was very excited about the whole thing. I didn't know what to expect but nothing had prepared me for the work ahead or the extent of it all. Anyone who thinks it's a week of partying has another think coming. There are parties, of course, but if you don't do your research beforehand you're in for a shock when you sit in the commentator's box with three hours of live commentary to do.

There's a most important meeting called the commentators' briefing when you're told how to pronounce all the names of the singers and songwriters – that can be challenging.

When Colm Wilkinson sang for Ireland in 1978 it was one of the most exciting moments of my career. I presented The National Song Contest when Shay Healy won with Johnny Logan singing *What's Another Year?* In 1980, I was the TV commentator and remember feeling so proud when the song won. The Irish delegation painted the town red. I did the next two years as the TV commentator. Ireland didn't have an entry in 1983, and in 1984 I did the radio commentary and continued to do radio coverage for the next twenty-nine years.

For some of these last years Julian Vignoles was the Head of Delegation. Then he got elected to the committee that 'bosses' the Heads of Delegation (meetings in nice cities I gather!) and he knows more about the workings of Eurovision than any other person I know.

His book is a fascinating insight into everything about the Eurovision Song Contest – what you see and what you don't see, but would love to know all the goings on behind the scenes. For anyone interested in the Eurovision it's a must read. I just couldn't put it down. Julian was a brilliant Head of Delegation and when you read his book you'll be able to discuss every aspect of the Contest – like a pro!

I give this book 12 points!

Larry Gogan
Producer/Presenter at 2FM

Larry Gogan with Phil Coulter in Riga, 2003

Dedication

For Eurovision artists – and the fans

Introduction

An Irishman in Eurovision Land

We praise thee, O God:
we acknowledge thee to be the Lord.
All the earth doth worship thee:
the Father everlasting.
To thee all Angels cry aloud:
the Heavens, and all the Powers therein.
– From the *Te Deum* (the Book of Common Prayer)

Each year it begins and ends with an early Christian hymn of praise. But with or without the *Te Deum*, the Eurovision Song Contest's feast of pop must be doing something right to last nearly sixty years. Love it or laugh at it, for millions across Europe it's a great spectacle that comes their way every year just as summer is emerging. Thousands of fans will pay exorbitant hotel prices to stay for up to two weeks in the host city. Grand Final tickets cost hundreds of Euro. No touring music act can compete with it as a premium event.

It's also a proven survivor of crises. In 1969 when the voting system allowed four countries to tie for first place, some participants opted out in protest. In the early years of this century, many in the west condemned the ESC as 'an East European Contest'. And in 2006, some thought the end was near following the victory of the hard-rock 'monsters' from Finland, Lordi – the Contest would 'never be taken seriously

1

again'. Instead, it gave this television monster, the 1950s brainchild of a Director General of Swiss Television, Marcel Bezençon, another boost.

I enjoyed working behind the scenes of the Eurovision Song Contest in various roles from 2003 to 2012. This book is not a complete history, with year-by-year facts – John Kennedy O'Connor has done that in his official history.[1] This behind-the-scenes book is a combination of personal observations and reflections, along with some explanation of the important changes that took place in that period of Eurovision's history. In looking at how it works, I also touch on some misconceptions about the Eurovision.

A show as extravagant as Eurovision is bound to create enduring memories …

In Düsseldorf in 2011, two Dublin brothers, John and Edward Grimes, known to the world as Jedward, high-fived and cartwheeled as the backing singers kept the vocals going. Then, with four seconds left, the confetti-cannon fired. As the little pieces of multi-coloured plastic floated back down to the stage and the backing-track ended, a camera directly in front of the stage caught the twins through the falling glitter as the crowd erupted. The cheer got louder, as if fanning the out-of-focus confetti. It was a great moment; we all thought we were going to win.

But the Eurovision is about disappointment as well as triumph. Each May, up to forty countries *lose* the Contest, as a TV producer friend, Darren Smith, said after his act, Dustin, was badly beaten in Belgrade in 2008. The truth is that one-third of the countries now regularly competing in the competition have never won it. Of the remainder, only ten have won more than once since the first competition in Lugano, Switzerland in 1956.

As an ESC insider, I saw the way different people handle both victory and defeat – and sometimes in their disappointment they imagine conspiracies to do regions or countries down. It's not just about the drama of *douze* or *nul* points, but the awarding of the all-important

---

[1] *50 Years: The Official History of the Eurovision Song Contest*, Carlton Books, 2010

A group of 'Jedheads' celebrate their heroes' qualification for the final in 2011. Diarmuid Furlong, Irish Fan Club chairman, is centre, left.

fifty-eight points, the total number each country, big or small, has to give, that generates so much heat.

The format is simple, but enduring; each country gets their three minutes to shine – or not. There are basic rules that haven't changed for decades: six persons is the maximum allowed on the stage, and all vocals must be live. The songs must not be longer than three minutes and must not have been performed or commercially released prior to a specific cut-off date, currently September 1 of the year preceding each Contest. The Eurovision Song Contest is controlled by the European Broadcasting Union (the EBU), through a board, called the Reference Group, and an Executive Supervisor.

Behind the scenes you observe, as well as participants' human nature, the elaborate planning, the mishaps and the controversies, the carefully considered rule changes, that all help to keep the Contest a great 'appointment to view', even in the increasingly competitive media environment. Eurovision combines music and glamour (some might say tackiness) with state-of-the-art television. It's sport too. And it's unpredictable.

It can be humbling too. Artists can falter under the pressure. There's no chance to start the song again, or sing a different song. It can be lonely out there; up to 100 million people are judging you. The songwriter and arranger Phil Coulter once used a taxi metaphor: 'Once you're on that stage, the meter is ticking.'

I got the Eurovision 'bug' in Istanbul in 2004 and it's never left me. It's the excitement, the glamour, the spectacle, the show's unique combination of music and sport. I was Head of Delegation for Ireland for seven Contests. I was elected twice to the Reference Group, the Contest's governing body, and served on it between 2006 and 2011. The results we achieved in that period were similar to most countries. They pale in comparison to Ireland's 'winning streak' in the 1990s and our seven-victory unequalled record, but there are several factors for that which I'll also discuss.

My first experience of Eurovision was chastening. I sat in the green room at the final in Turkey on 15 May 2004 as country after country gave points to everyone except Ireland. It wasn't till we got to the UK jury that we got something, seven points, our only ones that night. We came twenty-third out of twenty-four – Norway was on the bottom. The organisers were generous with the champagne, but it just didn't taste good in the circumstances.

Brian McFadden, the writer of the Irish entry, *If My World Stopped Turning,* chain-smoked throughout the voting. Phil Coulter, Ireland's musical director that year, couldn't get over it. It was a big comedown for him as he had been in the winner's enclosure with Sandie Shaw in 1967, co-writing *Puppet on a String.* And, but for the Spanish dictator Franco's intervention the following year (according to one theory), he would have been there with Cliff Richard and *Congratulations,* when they were nudged into second place by one point after the last jury delivered. More about that later…

But that night in the Abdi Ipecki Arena, we all thought Chris Doran had done well. I discovered soon after his performance that that wasn't necessarily the view back home. I got a call from a friend – an expert on traditional Irish singing – who asked, 'What happened? He was completely off key.' We had all been too caught up in the 'bubble' that is Eurovision to notice. There was a lesson in that: You really have to stand back and try to assess everything you're doing objectively. At the same time you have to, of necessity, wear your 'country's colours'.

Chris always maintained that his earpiece had slipped out, causing him to lose the sound of his own voice. In fairness, Chris had been a stellar singer in the *You're a Star* competition that had selected him. The mood that night wasn't helped by the song's chorus, which ended with the words, '...a winner out of me'.

Ukraine won with *Wild Dances,* performed memorably by Ruslana (also known as 'Xena: Warrior Princess') and her backing group in matching 'designer cave-woman' costumes. Serbia and Montenegro came second. Suggestions of 'eastern bloc voting' were heard and there was anger back home. I never accepted this conspiracy view, firstly because I could see from the scoreboard that Ireland had given Ukraine seven points. *Wild Dances* had received points from all countries except Switzerland. There were no real excuses; the Ruslana act was, truthfully, in a different league to our effort, as was the Serbian song, a power ballad that opened with an exhilarating thirty-second violin solo.

Some believe that going on an ESC delegation is a kind of junket, a fortnight of partying. There are parties of course, if you're able for them. But the pressure on delegations in the Eurovision cauldron is relentless – logistics to be planned, endless arrangements, costumes, interviews, everything to be negotiated in a strange city. Then there are nerves, tantrums, bad time keeping and sometimes health issues to contend with for a Head of Delegation. It requires a cool head – and plenty of energy. People are constantly 'in your ear' with their suggestions about every detail. There's a lot of waiting – minutes, hours, days – because there are dozens of acts to be rehearsed and only one stage. I remember the long waits. In Athens, I was pacing the floor as we waited in the dressing room area for the show to begin. Brian Kennedy said to me, 'Julian, you seem very nervous. But *I'm* the one who should have the nerves!'

And let's remember this is television entertainment, celebrating the magic of novelty and surprise. In 2012, six elderly women from a small village, Buranovo, in Russia's Udmurtia region east of the Volga River, dressed in traditional costume, looking like they'd just finished milking their cows, represented that vast country. They performed *Party for Everybody* partly in their native dialect, and the women from the steppes with their wistful harmonies seemed completely unfazed by the big stage. To some it may have seemed a joke, but it wasn't. Buranovskiye Babushki, the 'Russian Grannies', won their semi-final, and picked up 259 points in the final, to finish second. Producing surprises has always been a Eurovision asset.

There have been academic studies of the ESC – attempts to connect it with the political evolution of Europe, and 'sociological' theories about particular countries and the relationship between a Contest entry and a country's economic fortunes. But such connections, at the end of the day, are difficult to prove. And the language used can become obtuse: Brian Singleton, of Trinity College Dublin, looked at recent Irish involvement in an essay in 2013 titled 'From Dana to Dustin: The Reputation of Old/New Ireland and the Eurovision Song Contest', has this to say:

> Reputation is a measure of trust with regard to the value of the performance of a past behavior that enables the prediction of a future performative behavior. Rather than simply reflecting the past, a reputation is a show of the future, operating in the present.[2]

---

[2] *Performing the 'New' Europe*, edited by Karen Fricker and Milija Gluhovic, Palgrave MacMillan, 2013

Jedward and Babanovskiye Babuski (the 'Russian Grannies'), in Baku, Azerbaijan, in 2012. There was a view that the elderly women had been 'created' for Eurovision, but they already had a career singing traditional songs and also covers of standards like Hotel California *and* Let It Be.

Dustin's reaction to this would be interesting, but probably unprintable. Perhaps the Contest is intriguing enough without resorting to such analysis, yet it elevates and even flatters the event, too. Dr. Aileen Dillane, a lecturer at the Irish World Academy of Music and Dance at the University of Limerick, looks at it this way:

> There is no no such thing as 'just entertainment'. Popular music is the music of our lives. It says so much about our value systems, our tastes and preferences, the manner in which the industry is controlled, the way in which a song can surprise and lift you.

Niall Mooney, who co-wrote two of Ireland's recent entries, has a songwriter's judgment:

> What I love about the Eurovision is that this contest allows any songwriter who has a dream to have their music heard all

around the world a platform to achieve that. I think the worst thing for me is the cynicism I listen to from people who just don't think it's cool enough. Lighten up and just go with it.

The Eurovision definitely has its critics. Terry Wogan, the BBC's Eurovision commentator for many years – and he had some great lines in mocking various performers – in his latter years took a view that there was some kind of takeover by the East, and in doing so, I believe, promoted some untruths about the Contest. It was striking to me that Irish-born Wogan, a very clever and funny man, played not only to a cynicism in Britain about the Contest, but also to a somewhat chauvinistic view of its European neighbours. More about Sir Terry later.

Yet the Contest's survival is partly due to another aspect of nationalist feeling – the pride that comes into play when a country wins, followed usually by a willingness to host the increasingly expensive event – often elaborately.

Eurovision is about so much more than 'good' and 'bad' songs; it's about great debates, voting, juries, costumes – and little incidents. In 2009 there was a small 'cufflinks crisis'. When the multi-millionaire composer Andrew Lloyd Webber graced the Eurovision final in Moscow to accompany his song, *It's My Time,* sung by Jade Ewen, a small detail caused a last minute hitch to the elaborate plans. I was with Marty Whelan in our commentary box high up in the stadium when the BBC producer, Helen Tumbridge, who was working with Graham Norton in the adjoining booth, came to us in a panic – Andrew had forgotten the cufflinks for his shirt. Could I help? There was no time for someone to go back to his posh hotel, given the Moscow traffic. I just couldn't let the BBC down. So one of popular music's greats, a good way to being a billionaire, wore my shirt accessories as his arms moved across the (muted) keys. I just had to roll up my sleeves for the night.

In this cauldron of multi-megawatts of lights, passions are aroused and predictions confounded. Kjell Eckholm, a Finnish ESC veteran, can't forget the morning after the Lordi victory in Athens when a se-

*'Beauty and the Beast': Backstage in Athens, 2006. Una Healy, now Una Foden,
a backing singer for Ireland that year, went on to fame as a member of
The Saturdays, and became a coach on The Voice of Ireland in 2015.*

nior European Broadcasting Union (EBU) executive came to him and said:

> ... you have destroyed this great competition with these monsters! They should never have won and it will be a disaster next year because then we will have lots of similar ones taking part in it.

And in comes a simple innovation for the 2015, the sixtieth ESC – just add … Australia.

I love the Eurovision Song Contest. Millions do. Others love hating it. It's that unique combination of glamour, music and myth.

Molly Sterling, Ireland's hope for Eurovision 2015
(Photo: Andres Poveda)

Chapter 1

The Dresses, the Fans and the Songs: The Sixty-Year Legacy

John Kennedy O'Connor, in his book, *50 Years: The Official History of the Eurovision Song Contest,* describes it as 'possibly the most controversial and maligned television show ever broadcast in the world'.

A Eurovision cliché is that it 'brings Europe together'. Graham Norton was mocking this, perhaps, as he previewed the Moscow Contest with a quip: 'Cheap vodka and an unintelligible language. What could possibly go wrong?'

The passion of its hard-core fans is arguably the cement that binds Eurovision. They are known of course to be mostly male, predominantly of one sexual orientation and most have Eurovision statistics, trivia and historic minutiae at their fingertips. They never tire of flying their countries' flags with gusto. They'll go online at the slightest hint of news. An impending rule change will eat up cyberspace. They will analyse songs, costumes and even hairstyles well into the early hours. 'The brotherhood of Eurovision obsessives is populous and ever swelling,' Tim Moore, an English travel writer, put it in 2006, in his sarcastic tone. He was on a 'journey' to track down the thirteen (at that stage) singers 'who had suffered the entertainment world's prime humiliation' – they got no points. Moore's observation of the fans continued:

Theirs, happily, is no jealously guarded passion: after no more than a tentative paddle into the vast ocean that is the pool of their online knowledge, I'd discovered that two contestants have been the grandchildren of Nobel laureates, that Iceland and Greece have both entered songs entitled *Socrates,* that when Abba triumphed at the Dome in Brighton, they did so without a single vote from the UK jury.[3]

Petra Mede, the Swedish comedienne who presented the 2013 Eurovision in Malmö, joked pointedly during one of the shows:

This audience is full of men, they must have all left their wives at home?

Diarmuid Furlong, President of the Irish branch of OGAE,[4] who has attended fourteen Contests, puts the 'gay fest' label in perspective, admitting its truth:

The Irish Eurovision Fan Club has about 250 members, of which 45 are women, 25 are heterosexual men, we have one lesbian member and the other 179 are gay men. So yes, I guess it is a bit of a gay fest!

He admits a few things about his Eurovision fellow travellers:

Just like fans of anything, football, tennis, Star Trek, stamp collecting, you are going to get a very mixed bunch of individuals. You do get those nerdy anoraks that will know every minute detail of every Contest, from singer to performer, from points received to costumes worn. But the majority of fans are there because they love everything about the Contest and they are there to have a good time.

Michael Kealy, the RTÉ person now in charge of Ireland's Eurovision effort, has a theory that a lot of the hard-core fans are not really music fans, but have more in common with train-spotters:

---

[3] *Nul Points*, Tim Moore, Vintage, 2006.

[4] Organisation Générale des Amateurs de l'Eurovision (General Organisation of Eurovision Fans) is an international organization founded in 1984

They love statistics and the bragging rights they get from being able to say they were at this rehearsal or that rehearsal, they love cataloguing things like train-spotters. It's not about the songs or the music, it's inevitably about the big hair and the dresses and the glamour and glitz. The sheer scale of the show makes it an addictive experience for the average Entertainment TV producer, so I can only imagine what affect it has on them.

The fans are great to have on your side in Eurovision's pressurised, competitive theatre. I remember being backstage and hearing the spontaneous cheer from the small Irish contingent in the giant Olympic Indoor Hall in Athens in 2006 when Brian Kennedy went down on one knee to sing the last verse of *Every Song Is a Cry for Love*. Word had come from home that the one knee idea didn't work. I disagreed, and

Brian Kennedy on bended knee in Athens, 2006

so did the Irish contingent in the hall. (Incidentally, Brian Kennedy had gone into the record books that moment as Eurovision's 1,000th performer.)

Diana Mnatsakanyan, who was in charge of Armenia's participation in the Contest for five years, recalls a typical Eurovision fan scenario:

> There were times when my last piece of promotional material went to one fan and the other ones surrounding me in a circle felt offended and really heartbroken. They could burst with tears and it embarrassed me a lot, so I had to hug them, apologise and find ways to soothe.

To remind us of the basics, this is how the competitive part of the Eurovision Song Contest works: There are two semi-finals and a final. A semi-final was introduced in 2004 to deal with the number of countries wanting to take part. This was expanded to two semis in 2008. All countries must take part in a semi-final, except the 'Big Five' (Germany, France, the UK, Spain and Italy) and the country hosting. After the songs are performed, viewers in the countries participating in the the semi-finals, are invited to vote for their favourite songs (except for the song representing their own country) by means of televoting. In addition, each participating country has a national jury. The procedure in the Eurovision final is the same except that all countries participating, including those not reaching the final, participate in the voting.

In the televoting, the song that has received the highest number of votes is ranked first; the song receiving the second highest number of votes is ranked second and so on until the last song. In each national jury's voting, the jury members rank their favourite song first, their second favourite song, second, third, and so on to their least favourite song, which is then ranked last.

The rankings of the televoting and the jury are then, in each of the participating countries, used to calculate the average rank of each song. This combined ranking is then transformed to the familiar Eurovision points system, with the top-ranked song getting twelve points, the second-highest ranked song ten points, and the remaining spots, from eight points to one point, given to the songs ranked three to ten. Of course, no voting system, or procedure for deciding a winner of anything – whether artistic or sporting – is perfect. The ESC voting and its controversies will be dealt with in more detail in Chapter 2.

So if it's a 'European' event, the question is often asked 'how come Israel, and countries like Armenia and Azerbaijan are involved?' The answer is that these states are only one of many 'non-mainland Europe' countries that are entitled to apply to participate. Egypt, Algeria, Tunisia and Libya could all apply, as they are European Broadcasting Union members. The EBU's website states:

> Active membership is open to authorized broadcasting organisations from countries which are either within the European Broadcasting Area (as defined by the International Telecommunication Union) or, if their country is outside that area, are members of the Council of Europe.

Morocco actually joined the Contest in 1980, came eighteenth, but hasn't been back since. Lebanon's stop-start relationship with the ESC is dealt with in Chapter 8.

On occasions, war has been the backdrop to the Eurovision show. In 1993, hostilities were on going in Bosnia and Herzegovina when the Contest was staged in the Irish countryside, in Millstreet, the smallest host town ever for the show. Applause rang out round the hall as a voice on a distant-sounding phone line said, 'Hello Millstreet, Sarajevo calling'. The moment perhaps recalled, nearly forty years on, one of the founding purposes of the ESC – to bring Europe together peacefully. Now with communist Eastern Europe dissolving, Yugoslavia, which had traditionally been the only communist country to take part in the Contest, was no more. One of its regions, Bosnia and Herzegovina, was making its bid for a place in the world community.

The EBU had to deal with this sudden explosion in the number of potential competing countries. As well as Bosnia and Herzegovina that year, Hungary, Slovenia, Slovakia, Romania and Estonia all wanted in.

The solution chosen was to let these countries battle it out in a special competition in Ljubljana in April for three places available at the final in Millstreet. After some extremely tight voting, Bosnia and Herzegovina, Croatia and Slovenia edged through.

So 'Hello Millstreet, Sarajevo calling' was not just a greeting from a city under siege, but heralded a fresh era for Eurovision. New countries were eagerly 'marching west' – musically and metaphorically – and would later make a significant mark on the Contest.

So, some devotees' facts and curiosities: Which four countries tied at the top and in what year? Easy if you're a real fan: France, Spain, Netherlands, and the UK in 1969. As a protest against this mess-up, Austria, France, Sweden, Norway and Portugal refused to participate the following year.

In 1973, backing tracks were permitted for the first time, though the orchestra survived another twenty-five years. Who was the first artist to use a recorded track, also known as singing to 'playback'? Cliff Richard with *Power to All Our Friends.* Cliff's song produced another piece of Eurovision trivia: The lyrics contained a solecism (bad grammar) where it described a girl as 'laying down in Monte Carlo', instead of 'lying down'. For the live performance of the song at the Eurovision final, the BBC's Director General, Bill Cotton apparently requested that Cliff sing the correct English 'lying down in Monte Carlo'. At any rate, the 'a' remained in the 'laying down' when he performed it in the Grand Theatre, Luxembourg.

Nostalgia is strong among followers of the Contest, the orchestra featuring strongly in this. A conductor and musicians in evening dress would seem totally out of place with video-walls and floors, but some, including the veteran Linda Martin, miss the men and women with the sheet music. As recently as 2010, there was a Facebook campaign to bring them back in the run-up to the Oslo Contest. That somewhat 'retro' wish is also shared by Niamh Kavanagh:

I would bring back the orchestra if I got my wish; I know it's not a practical thing, but I love musicians and live music. And it brings challenges that tracks don't.

Is there a language rule? Not any more. Countries used to be obliged to sing in a national language (some countries have more than one). When was the rule changed? Three times. In 1973, 1977 and 1999. So the rule allowed Abba to sing in English in 1974. Ireland and the UK, with one-fifth of all winners between them, haven't won the competition since everybody else could 'borrow' the English language. Almost half of all Contest wins, twenty-eight, have been songs sung in English.

Stefan Raab, Germany's mercurial Eurovision veteran during part of his colourful presentation of the Eurovision in Düsseldorf in 2011

Eurovision has had its fair share of 'mercurial characters': Stefan Raab is just one; a television host, comedian, and musician, considered the 'most powerful man in German entertainment television'. Raab also produced, wrote and performed German entries for Eurovision. He was involved in the organisation of the national pre-selection, 'Our Star for Oslo', which led to Germany's winning entry at the 2010 Contest, Lene, who he managed. He went on to jointly present the Düsseldorf show.

Germany also has a songwriter who never gave up. The charming veteran Ralph Siegel from Munich has been involved in 21 songs – so far, the latest being the 2014 San Marino entry, *Maybe*, sung by Valentina Monetta. In 1982, Siegel and Bernd Meinunger's song, *A Little Peace*, performed by Nicole won the Contest and became a hit in Europe and is still a staple in many a church. In 2010, he qualified for Ireland's selection with *River of Silence*, performed by Lee Bradshaw. It ended in last place.

Much has been made over the years by fans and commentators about a country's position in the running order. The wisdom is that early or late is best. Some fans get seriously worked up about this, but the truth is songs have won and lost from all positions on the starting grid. It may be an advantage to come towards the end closer to when the voting starts, but an act has to stand out from what's gone before it for that to work, as Ireland, for example, discovered when they came last in Copenhagen in 2013, after performing in the coveted last slot.

For the Contest's all-important fan base, a subversive lifestyle statement came courtesy of a non-European, a Tel Aviv-born singer, officially male until shortly before taking to the Eurovision stage in 1998, Sharon Cohen, otherwise known as Dana International. She was the first transsexual to enter the Contest, and took the name from Ireland's 1970 winning singer. In Israel there were protests at her selection. At the Eurovision, security – and hype – was all part of the package. By all accounts she didn't sing particularly well in Birmingham, but her stage presence and confidence won the night. She dispensed with the orchestra, the first winner not to use any live music. Gay fans adored her. She inspired discourse around gender and sexuality. A new era of the Contest had begun. Gay men were attracted to the Eurovision long before that year, Linda Martin recalls, noticing their enthusiasm when she first competed in 1984 with *Terminal 3*.

> It's the foolishness of the Contest, the crazy costumes and stage productions that has attracted a fun-loving element. The difference is that people can be more openly gay now.

History was to some extent repeated in Copenhagen sixteen years later in 2014, when Conchita Wurst, a transvestite rather than a transsexual, triumphed with her gentle take on the expression of sexuality, charming Europe enough to give Austria its first win since 1966. But there were critics, too. The Armenian singer, Aram Mp3, was one who couldn't appreciate the act and said Conchita's lifestyle was 'not natural' and she needed to decide to be a woman or a man. He later apologised, saying he was joking. The Lithuanian spokesperson, Ignas Krupavičius, just before announcing that ten points of his country's vote had been assigned to Conchita Wurst, said referring to Wurst's beard, 'Now it is time to shave', then pulled out a razor and pretended to shave his own face, before giggling at his joke. The presenter, Nikolaj Koppel, replied to that by saying, 'Time to shave? I think not.'

In the UK later in February 2015, *The Telegraph* reported that several church leaders had claimed recent devastating flooding across the Balkans, which was the worst in a century and left over fifty people dead, was divine punishment for Conchita's victory. 'This [flood] is not a coincidence, but a warning,' Patriarch Amfilohije of Montenegro said. 'God sent the rains as a reminder that people should not join the wild side.' Patriarch Irinej, the spiritual leader of Eastern Orthodox Serbs, reportedly said that 'God is thus washing Serbia of its sins'.

Costumes – good, bad and indifferent – are a major part of the appreciation of the Eurovision phenomenon. They can often get as much analysis as the songs. I remember hours and hours of discussion about what our Irish performers would be wearing and what was wrong with the colour or style of a particular outfit. Every delegation seemed to have anxious deliberation about this highly subjective issue. Ireland's singer in 2009, Sinéad Mulvey, had a rather expensive dress provided for her, but refused to wear it for the show after her mother saw a rehearsal on Eurovision.tv and told her daughter she 'looked fat'. I had the pleasure of working with patient, professional wardrobe colleagues over the years, such as Brigette Horan, Catherine Manning and Helen McCusker. On this occasion, Helen, Sinéad and myself walked around the hot Moscow streets looking for a replacement. A tutu type number was eventually chosen, but in the next rehearsal the wind ma-

Sinéad Mulvey and Black Daisy with their 'rock chick' look. They came eleventh in their semi-final in Moscow in 2009, narrowly missing the final.

chine that was used to blow Sinéad's (and other singers') hair caused the bottom of the skirt to blow upwards – rather revealingly. A cheap 'rock chick' tee shirt and leggings was the final choice. There were no complaints.

In 2010, there was another Irish dress issue, which also arose after a rehearsal was seen. It involved a dressmaking firm from Dublin who were under the impression that their dress would be the one used by Niamh Kavanagh. But we had decided, based on how two competing garments looked on the stage in Oslo, to use the other one for the shows. The story was

Sinéad Mulvey

all over the papers. People in RTÉ were getting worked up. I remember at what appeared to be the height of the controversy, the day before our semi-final, Sharon Brady, our press officer, and myself were wearily grabbing a coffee in the stadium when the phone rang again. The voice at the other end was a senior RTÉ person: 'How did you manage it?', he asked. 'How do you mean?', I replied, expecting to be told off. 'How did you manage to get such great publicity on the day before the show?' Even allowing a little for irony, it was such a relief.

The 'House of Eurovision' fan-site hosts a Barbara Dex Award each year. The prize is a gong for the worst dressed artist in the Contest. It's named after Barbara Dex, who represented Belgium in the 1993, and came last wearing her self-designed dress – regarded by those-who-know as awful. Where else would you get it?

'My dress from Malmö still fits me', says Linda Martin proudly, speaking of her legendary garment. It's twenty-five years since she first wore it for her winning performance with *Why Me?* in 1992. 'But I can't quite get the zip at the back up the whole way,' she admits. Paul Moreland, a milliner, made the legendary garment. He got to hear that a special dress was needed and decided to pitch to RTÉ as a dress-maker. 'It's made of curtain velvet, it's not even dress fabric, but it's a beautiful dress, very intricately made.' Martin brought it with her to Baku in 2012 and could be seen surrounded by fans admiring its folds and stitching detail.

The biggest change since seven nations competed in the small Theatro Kursaal in Lugano in 1956 was the technology of televoting. It was assumed by many that introducing it was driven by revenue, but there

Verka Serduchka, Ukraine's singer in Helsinki in 2007, enjoying a few tunes from Dervish, Ireland's representatives that year.

Una Healy tries out her songwriting on Brian Kennedy
in the dressing room in Athens.

was more to it. Firstly, the public being allowed to choose the winner rather than some unseen individuals seemed a more democratic option. As well as this, juries had, it was argued, become somewhat out of touch with popular taste. The Irish win in 1996 is a case in point: *The Voice* was different, atmospheric, but certainly not pop and, though all credit is due to Eimear Quinn and her ensemble for standing out among the glitter with Brendan Graham's song, it was not the popular choice, as John Kennedy O'Connor related:

> The result was not appreciated much in the hall, with many leaving their seats before Eimear Quinn had even begun her reprise. As the credits rolled, the EBU were obviously taking notes. By electing Ireland winners again, the juries may well have confirmed their own demise.[5]

---

[5] *50 Years: The Eurovision Song Contest Official History,* John Kennedy O'Connor, Carlton, 2005.

So when did televoting begin? In 1997 five countries decided to experiment with this new idea. It caught on. And usually once you give the vote to the people, there's no going back. But, in fact, there was 'going back' – juries were to make a return in a new 50/50 formula in the 2009 Contest.

And that's the one issue that puts the clothes, and even the songs, in the shade – the infamous voting.

Happy Delegation: Left to Right, backing singers Una Healy, Paula Gilmer, and Fran King, producer Calum McColl, Bridgette Horan from RTÉ Wardrobe, and singer Brian Kennedy. In front, Sharon Brady, press officer for Ireland and right, myself. There had been tensions in the run-up to the Contest that year. The submitted songs were considered not good enough by the song selection judges, RTÉ, and Brian Kennedy; the closing date was extended, after which Brian submitted his own song, Every Song is a Cry for Love. *This was by agreement and entirely in keeping with the rules. Vindication came with qualification from the semi-final and tenth place in the final that year.*

At the Acropolis: Brian Kennedy, with backing singers Una Healy, Paula Gilmer and Fran King, and Calum McColl, the producer of Every Song is a Cry for Love. *He's a son of the English folk singer, songwriter and activist Ewan McColl and stepbrother of Kirsty McColl.*

Chapter 2

A Continent Gets Worked Up: The Voting

'The voting is outrageous, unfair…it's political…'
'The best song always wins…'

These two views summarise the spectrum of opinion on Eurovision voting. In the end, because winners and losers have to be decided, perhaps it will always generate debate. But the facts and analysis I will outline here will certainly surprise many who may have suspected 'foul play' over the years in this, the sport of Eurovision.

'How many more countries have we got? What time is it?' said the BBC's commentator, Terry Wogan, from his box high up in the Palace of Sports in Kiev, Ukraine. Russia had just given their points, the thirty-fifth country to do so. It didn't take much for Wogan to be sarcastic about the Contest, but perhaps this time he had a point. At just under three and a half hours it became the longest final ever. Russia, incidentally, had given their highest points that year to 'neighbours', Moldova and Belarus, which would probably have been a contributing factor to Wogan's irritation. As it turned out, it was the last year that all points were announced by each country's spokesperson; from the Athens Contest the following year on, points one to seven are delivered electronically.

For many millions of viewers, the voting is the most exciting part of the Eurovision, and a ratings winning part of the show. It's also the most discussed, controversial – and, I feel, misunderstood.

Firstly, many people are not aware of the basic, founding principle of the Contest – that all countries, big and small, have the same voting power. Russia with its huge population and size, and the island of Malta, a small territory, each has the same points to give. Fifty-eight. That's when points one, two, three, four, five, six, seven and eight are added to the famous ten and twelve.

Many in the West have made the accusation of 'bloc voting' in the Contest. The Balkan countries and Scandinavia have been judged guilty. The worst offenders, however, the theory goes, are the countries formerly under Soviet influence. Contest commentators from the West in their broadcasts often suggested this, and 'political voting' as an explanation to their audience when few points were being awarded to their song.

The background to this was the huge expansion in the number of qualifying countries joining the Contest after the fall of Communism. Europe was 'expanding' eastwards and many in 'old Europe' were somewhat uncomfortable. That these 'new' countries should triumph in popular music and stagecraft was not expected. Many commentators in the West didn't appear to recognise that there was diversity in 'former communist Europe'. *The Guardian* is highly regarded in Britain as a newspaper of record, yet it's rock and pop columnist, Caroline Sullivan, could write in 2007, as she accused eastern countries of cheating and collusion:

> ... you wouldn't go broke betting that representatives of all 15 eligible states are huddled in a conference room in the Carpathians as we speak, discussing tactics.

The music itself has to be remembered in this discussion. Countries like Ukraine, Armenia, Romania and Moldova came to the Contest with inventive presentation, passion and polish. And they got good placings. I remember one UK fan's comment to me in the Eurovision

Press Centre in 2007: 'Eastern Europe are sometimes doing better because they often *are* better!'

Neighbour voting, between countries that share a border, has always been a feature of the Contest. It doesn't decide who wins or loses, however. The truth is that even if a country has a group of neighbours voting for their song, it neither proves a conspiracy nor enables winning of the Contest. Eurovision winners and runners-up will finish at the top of the scoreboard because they got points from all over the continent – east, west, north and south.

The 'friendliest' of neighbours might give its neighbour twelve points. So if we suppose that four countries give a particular neighbour maximum points (though it has rarely happened) that total of forty-eight points is still less than twenty per cent of what you need to win, based on the example of 2008 winner, Dima Bilan, and his (relatively modest) winning score of 272 points.

The conspiratorial view assumes there's a political element to the neighbour voting. This doesn't acknowledge that regional taste, familiarity with an artist, or shared TV channels might all be more relevant factors. And there's an even simpler explanation: some countries just have more appealing songs. Ukraine is worth examining in this context. They are consistently successful; in twelve attempts (up to 2015), they have won once, always qualified from the semi-finals and finished outside the top ten on only four occasions in that period. Why? Some fans have said it's because of their geographical position. My own view is that a more relevant factor is that Ukraine have consistently had a polished presentation of song and singer; in other words, a straight forward musical explanation for their above average success. They have supporting neighbours (countries they share a border with), but so have Poland and Belarus, both of whom have struggled in the Contest.

If we take the Ukraine's vote that year, 2008, where they qualified for the final and finished in second place, it breaks down as follows: in their semi-final, they received a total of 152 points. Former communist bloc countries (twenty-two out of a total of forty-three participating) gave them a total of ninety points; all other countries gave them sixty-two points. In the final they received 230 points, coming second. The breakdown was similar: 138 points from the 'east', with ninety-two points coming from 'old Europe' (this figure includes Turkey, Greece and Israel). The song, *Shady Lady*, sung by Ani Lorak, was getting points from all over the continent. The different east-west proportion in the figures, though clear, is not as dramatic as some might have guessed and could be accounted for by regional taste.

'Bloc voting' would also imply some kind of pre-arrangement by two or more countries to vote a certain way. This would be difficult enough to accomplish in a jury system, but virtually impossible with televoting. Yet still the accusation persisted for many years, and still does to a smaller extent. But if the 'culprits' (as far as many in 'old' Europe are concerned) had been successful, then the former Communist countries would have more winners from their ranks. But, as of 2014, the facts below point to a different conclusion: Seven out of the last ten winners of the ESC have been Western European countries (in bold):

2014: **Austria**

2013: **Denmark**

2012: **Sweden**

2011: Azerbaijan

2010: **Germany**

2009: **Norway**

2008: Russia

2007: Serbia

2006: **Finland**

2005: **Greece**

Of the Contest's ten winners that preceded these, only Ukraine, Latvia and Estonia could be counted as East European (Turkey, who won in 2003, is to the east geographically of course, but politically aligned with the West since 1945). So with only six winners since 1995, the

'East', far from dominating the Contest, is actually under-represented, it could be argued.

Another useful analysis is to consider the top ten placed countries in the Contest over the years. If we take 2004, where an Eastern country, Ukraine, was the winner, the top ten finishers that year were the following:

1. Ukraine
2. Serbia
3. Norway
4. Turkey
5. Cyprus (joint)
5. Sweden (joint)
7. Albania
8. Germany
9. Bosnia and Herzegovina
10. Spain

Assuming Cyprus and Turkey aren't counted as Eastern Europe, it means that 'Western-aligned' Europe had six out of the first ten places. In 2005, there was 'balancing out' when six out of the top ten places went to former Communist countries. This was hardly a take-over by the East, however.

So where did the talk of eastern dominance come from? From the phenomenon of 'neighbour voting' and diaspora voting, firstly. We've all heard a spokesperson deliver their final points to a neighbour. But analysis of the results shows the 'neighbour voting' is mainly an irritation, rather than a game changer. There is strong evidence that it was the result of various diaspora and their motivation to vote for their 'home country'. Also, there is the phenomenon of Russian speakers who live in other states. Germany, for most years since televoting began, consistently gave high points to Turkey. But this didn't give Turkey a big advantage. Similarly, Spain gave consistently high points to Romania between 2004 and 2009, Romanians being a significant minority in Spain, but it had little bearing on Romania's result. And of course the United Kingdom and Ireland have helped each other over the years.

Secondly, there has been something of a bias against former Communist countries and their efforts at popular music by some western commentators – a kind of 'western chauvinism'. This, I believe, was partly a taste issue – what the East was producing musically didn't find favour in the Western end of the continent. This view was very prevalent in the UK, and expressed in Terry Wogan's commentary. Though undoubtedly witty, Wogan couldn't accept a musical explanation when the United Kingdom weren't getting votes. When the UK came last in Riga in 2003, he suggested that the UK was suffering from 'post-Iraq backlash'. But perhaps a more likely explanation is that the duo, Jemini, who weren't exactly a 'hot' act anyway, sang off key. John Kennedy O'Connor put it bluntly, after pointing out the statistics such as the fact that no song sung in English had ever before failed to score:

> Such was the tuneless and uninspired effort from the hapless duo that all these statistics were swept away by their inept performance.[6]

As in much of human history, disappointment and a blow to a nation's pride can breed conspiracy theories. Instead of looking to the song or the singer as the cause, Wogan tended to look to other countries' behavior. He appeared to even suggest after the Contest in Serbia in 2008, where Russia won for the first time, that it had been somehow 'arranged'. In *The Guardian* on 26 May, Steven Morris wrote:

> Later he [Terry Wogan] suggested it had been common knowledge that Russia was going to win. 'The word went out it was Russia's turn,' said Wogan.

---

[6] *50 Years: The Eurovision Song Contest Official History*. Carlton, 2005

Sir Terry also suggested, following the 2008 Contest, that countries that do not make it through the semi-finals should not be voting in the final. But if Terry had examined the scoreboard for the year he would have seen that the only votes the UK received were from countries that *weren't* in the final – San Marino and Ireland.

It was ironic that when the mantle was passed to Graham Norton for the Moscow Contest in 2009, the UK had its best result for seven years, coming fifth. As one fan said in the pressroom that year: 'All the UK had to do was show up with a decent song.' In the run-up to the selection of that year's entry, Andrew Lloyd Webber's song, *My Time,* Norton had gone to Russia to report for a BBC programme, part of the lead-up to the UK selection. He got an audience with Vladimir Putin, then prime minister of the country, who pointedly told him that 'in Russia we send our best performers, in Britain you don't'.

A strong neighbour-vote, even from several countries, can improve a country's position on the scoreboard, but it can't get a country into the contenders' list. If we take a very 'Eastern' year, 2007, and look at the top five countries (four out of five were former Communist states), we can see that there is a correlation, though it's not completely consistent, between the number of countries awarding that song/country votes and its final position on the scoreboard:

• Serbia got points from thirty-seven out of forty-one countries
• Ukraine got points from forty out of forty-one countries
• Russia got points from thirty-six countries
• Turkey got points from twenty-two countries
• Bulgaria got points from twenty-six countries

Then at the bottom, the fate of the last five: Spain had points from nine countries; Lithuania and France from five each; the UK got points from two countries, and Ireland, in last place, from one – Albania, ironically.

Scandinavia and Balkan countries are often rightly accused of 'neighbour voting'. However, staying with the 2007 results, we see that

Marty Whelan and friends, Athens 2006

Iceland, Denmark and Norway did not make it through to the final that year. Three from the Balkan region – Montenegro, Croatia and Albania – didn't qualify either. Returning to Scandinavia, Sweden only managed eighteenth place that year, despite high points from Norway, Finland, Iceland and Denmark. So neighbours aren't a lot of use if nobody else is interested in your song.

Many Western fans got annoyed about another aspect of 2007's Contest – the fact that only one western country, Turkey, qualified from the semi-final. That year was probably the peak of Eastern influence, because in what was a clean sweep, the former Communist part of the continent took nine of the top ten places. That's, of course, if you want to look at the results 'geopolitically'. Looking back at the songs themselves, however, might dispel any conspiracy theories. My own view is that it was the strength of the musical and theatrical appeal of certain songs that was the main reason for the result.

Would it be different if juries were deciding? Digame, the German company that manage the televote for the EBU, did an experiment that year, 2007, for the Reference Group. They took the televote and the juries' results (each country always had to have a backup jury in case the televote failed) and compared them. It revealed that the result in the final would have been much the same – the same winner, Serbia, and the same country coming last, Ireland. Germany's result was the most dramatic difference: sixth position with the juries, but nineteenth in the televote. Juries, mainly comprised of music professionals, were clearly taken with the jazz singer, Roger Cicero. Turkey, with a dance number, *Shake It*, came fourth in the televote, but ranked fourteenth with the juries. There was food for thought in the study, not to do with the East/West balance, but more to do with musical taste and the influence of a diaspora, that led to much debate in the Reference Group, culminating in the 50/50 jury and televote decision in 2009. I'll return to this in a later chapter.

Many new Eastern competitors put effort into the staging of their performances, making much of movement and colour and bringing a new dynamic to the Contest. They also brought a brand of pop with attractive ethnic musical motifs. From 2009 on, this influence waned, as 'older' countries copied much of the flamboyance. But the East had made its mark, even if some theatricality was over the top: In 2010 the Romanian act actually made sparks fly when their male-female duo Paula Seling and Ovi shot flames out of their sleeves; the Belarusian group 3+2 will be remembered for the climax of their song when they sprouted butterfly wings.

And of course there is no reason to assume that just because a particular song is doing well in the voting, and you don't like it yourself, that there's some kind of foul play afoot. Serbia and Russia won the competition in successive years with massive support from the former Eastern Europe. But the next year it seemed the same countries were queuing up to give Norway their twelve points for that country's record win.

The Eurovision viewers who vote must be given credit that the preferences they express are musical or performer motivated ones, rather than anything else. And yet it's hard for some to accept that. I

Larry Gogan, Louis Walsh and Marty Whelan in Düsseldorf, 2011.

remember having a de-brief back in Dublin after the 2012 Contest with the Irish commentator, Marty Whelan, who, during his witty and professional broadcast, couldn't hide his personal disappointment when Jedward and their song failed to have the same impact as they'd had in 2011. I recall saying to him: 'Remember that countries are perfectly entitled *not* to vote for us.'

There was much comment after recent Contests in the media and among fans at the jeering that often accompanies a spokesperson from Belarus or Ukraine giving their twelve points to Russia, or Andorra giving twelve to Spain, or Sweden to Norway. The reality is this neighbour voting is mostly just an irritation. And of course nobody in the UK or Ireland has ever objected to our two countries exchanging points. The damage was to the image of the Contest rather than to the credibility of the voting process. I'll return to this subject.

The victory in 2009 of a young Norwegian born in Belarus, Alexander Rybak, caused a lot of discussion behind the scenes in the EBU and the Reference Group. It wasn't because of his looks, or his song, or his violin's tuning. The problem was the margin of his victory.

Fairytale received a record-breaking 387 points out of a possible 492 (the total if all countries had given the song twelve points), Because he got so many countries' maximum points so early in the voting, the Contest was all over after fifteen minutes. But there was another hour left in the voting. How could the tension be brought back to this part of the show if this was to happen in the future?

A year later, a Swedish mathematician approached the EBU and the Norwegian broadcaster, NRK, with a solution. If it was known or could be predicted which countries were going to give their maximum points to the winner, then those scores should be kept till near the end of voting. In other words, postpone the inevitable as long as possible. He was also able to see to it that the country in the lead would change as often as possible. The mathematician would be given the information from Digame, crunch the numbers with his laptop, and then tell the host broadcaster in what order to call the countries to give their vote.

This is why, since 2011, the voting order is only decided the night before the final. It's based on the points awarded after the second dress rehearsal, called the 'Jury Final'. The observant viewer might have noticed that the twelve point scores for Azerbaijan that year all came towards the end of the voting.

But Sweden's victory with 113 points to spare the following year meant the Contest's new tweak had less impact than it might have had. There was little scope to 'engineer' a nail-biting finish, given Loreen's vote-getting ability. The six elderly Russian women, Buranovskiye Babushki, charmed the audience and got second place with

Alexander Rybak, the runaway winner for Norway in 2009

Party for Everybody, but the polished Swede with *Euphoria* ran away with it. That's Eurovision.

Many people analyse Eurovision voting. Adrian Kavanagh, a lecturer in Geography in Maynooth College and an Irish veteran of this pursuit, is particularly interested in the geographical aspect of the Contest. His sober number crunching has featured on several post

The joy of getting through a semi–final: Athens, 2006

mortems of Ireland's fortunes. He doesn't place much store in conspiracy theories either.

However, in the 2014 Contest, Kavanagh's well-argued theories left him somewhat off the mark in his predictions. In his blog (adriankavanagh.com) on 9 May, the day before the Final, he admitted, rightly I believe, that 'only a crystal ball can predict the quality and impact of the different acts' Eurovision Final performances at this stage', then went on to make a prediction based on 'past voting history, draw position and betting odds as a means of determining which countries are likely to do well in the 2014 Eurovision Final'. Combining what he called 'the voting bloc/history patterns' with the impact of draw position and the betting odd weightings, he predicted the following result:

Country	Points
Sweden	174
Greece	129
Armenia	121
Ukraine	115
Netherlands	114
Denmark	112
Azerbaijan	111
Austria	105

But the actual result was:

Country	Points
Austria	290
Netherlands	238
Sweden	213
Armenia	174
Hungary	143
Ukraine	113
Russia	89
Norway	88

The truth perhaps is that it is virtually impossible to predict the variables; the impression a singer is going to make on the night, or if their voice suddenly lets them down in their all-important three minutes. It's the mystery – the chemistry and magic of the performance – that gives Eurovision its unique drama.

The 'bloc voting' allegation can have its uses. I remember saying to a senior RTÉ colleague: 'You know, there's not much truth in this theory about bloc voting.' With a strategic mind, he replied: 'Do you know something, I'd keep that to yourself. It's useful that people believe all that when we come back with a bad result.'

And there is a somewhat ironic fact about Eurovision voting. The winner is actually known by a select group of people minutes after the voting closes. Software in Cologne sees to that. The giving of points by each country's spokesperson is pure television drama. The result *could* be announced instantly. But where would the fun be in that?

So, when the voting is finished, we have winners. And what happens to them all, when the celebrations are over?

The Netherlands had very poor results in the semi-final era of the Contest until this act came along, The Common Linnets. The 'country' duo took second place in the final in 2014 and followed it with chart success in several countries. The steadicam operator is seen on the right; most of the song was shot with this one camera circling round the singers. (photo: Albin Olsson)

Chapter 3

The Ups – and Downs – of Winning

Abba's mega-career following the Contest is the stuff of legend. Eurovision was a career launch pad on a scale never repeated by any other winner. They came to Brighton, England in 1974, for the nineteenth Contest, with *Waterloo,* styling themselves in the emerging fashion of glam-rock, and went on to mega-stardom. And getting no points from the UK jury didn't cause them to falter.

But one of the ESC's success stories in the last ten years, albeit modest in comparison, has been the Ukrainian singer, Ruslana. In the year following her victory in Istanbul in 2004, she charted in more than twelve countries. Her success, like several other winners, was mainly in the East, so she didn't get much in the way of acclaim – or even coverage – in the Western press.

The idea for the successful song, *Wild Dances*, began in her father's home place in western Ukraine, the land of the Hutsul people, natives of the Carpathian Mountains, a region shared by Ukraine and the northern extremity of Romania. Hutsuls have a semi-nomadic culture with an ancient and rich history, which apparently inspired Ruslana. The song's backing track is a triumph of the recording studio art, combining ethnic drums, the trumpet-like sounds of the trembita, an ancient Hutsul musical instrument, with modern dance beats. The track can still hold its own in a disco.

Ruslana, the 2004 winner

Ruslana was one of the leading figures of the pro-EU protests at Euromaidan, Independence Square, in 2013, after the Ukrainian government had suspended preparations for signing an Association Agreement with the European Union. She was honoured with several awards including the International Women of Courage Award, given by Michelle Obama at the Women in the World Summit in New York in 2014, the same year the singer organised a global prayer simulcast. Her involvement in Ukraine's turbulence continues.

Marija Šerifović, who won for Serbia in 2007, didn't have the same scale of success following her win as Ruslana, though perhaps had equal merits as a singer. Her winning song, *Molitva*, or 'Prayer', had passion, sweeping major to minor changes, a couple of notes that not many singers could reach, and was delivered with one of the best vocal performances of recent Contests.

Šerifović won in Helsinki, in the last of the single semi-final Contests. It was also well known for being the one where Western Europe performed poorly, with only one country qualifying for the final. But *Molitva* confounded conspiracy theorists, too: It was the first song containing no English language lyrics to win since Dana International's win for Israel in 1998 with *Diva*. As of 2014, it is also the last non-English song to win the ESC. It was also the first time a ballad has won since televoting became the standard. The song is also notable because it lacked dance routines, revealing or showy costumes or pyrotechnics. The Eurovision Song Contest is often accused of concentrating on these things instead of the music itself. The fact that *Molitva* contrasted so much with the previous winner, the Finns' Lordi and their *Hard Rock Hallelujah*, pointed to the Contest being much more open than some had believed.

And Marija, looking older than her twenty-two years, wore glasses – not even high fashion ones. But the backroom people in Belgrade had obviously addressed all this and she benefited from an exquisitely staged performance where five singers surrounded her, 'guiding' her – at one stage caressing her – through her performance.

The following year, 2008, she was a guest judge in the selection show in Ireland, held in the University of Limerick Concert Hall. It was the year of Dustin's participation. When the six competitors had all performed, the panel was asked for its opinions on the songs. Louis Walsh gave his verdict and the presenter then turned to Marija, who had been rather monosyllabic up till then. She paused, before pronouncing tersely, and mixing up her bird species, 'I think the duck has it!' Michael Kealy was the producer of the show and recalls her general demeanor:

Marija Šerifović with Dustin in Belgrade, 2008

After all five of our acts performed she took to the stage to do
a rendition of her winning song and she was a complete class
above any of our acts.

She had arrived in Limerick, attracted perhaps by the fee, Kealy
believes, with her manager and a male friend who she treated like a
pet dog:

He sat beside her looking adoringly at her while she stroked
him like you would a cat or dog.

In 2014 Marija Šerifović celebrated ten years in the music business
with a new record and an autobiography where she revealed a troubled
upbringing and alcoholic father. She also described herself as bisexual.

Perhaps because she sang it in her own language, *Molitva* only
made the top ten charts in two countries, Belgium and Sweden. But not

surprisingly, the song was often played for Serbia's sporting successes, featuring triumphantly at a welcome home party after Ana Ivanovic's French Open women's tennis singles victory in 2008. During 2007's Wimbledon, *Molitva* was taken for use in BBC clips displaying the courts and players, and heard before and after footage or interviews with the Serbian players.

There was also a fate element to this Serbian win in 2007. Despite having withdrawn from the 2006 Contest, Serbia and Montenegro (at the time still joined) retained their voting rights, and when announcing their votes that year their spokesperson, Jovana Janković was prophetic:

> So, as you know, we don't have a song for you this year, but
> we promise that next year we will give you the best one.

Her inadvertent prophecy was fulfilled by Šerifović the following year when Serbia entered as Serbia. And Janković also hosted the 2008 Contest in Belgrade.

In Helsinki in 2007, the Irish delegation had a regular driver from the official pool, a woman in her early forties who had taken leave from work to volunteer for the Contest. The work involved driving in heavy traffic and long hours. One day she was in particularly good form. 'It has all been worth it', she said. 'Why was that?' we wondered. 'Today I met Johnny Logan!'

It was further proof he wasn't called 'Mr. Eurovision' for nothing. He was in town as a guest of the broadcaster, YLE. He could still turn heads twenty years after his second record-breaking win. The Australian-born singer was also a hit songwriter, not only writing *Hold Me Now* for his second win, but also *Why Me?* for Linda Martin in 1992 and *Terminal 3*, which was a close runner-up in 1984.

Shay Healy, the writer of *What's Another Year*, the song that brought Logan his first victory, tells a self-deprecating story in his autobiography about a songwriter's fate (it's a *song* contest after all) in the immediate aftermath of the Irish victory in the Halle De Congress in The Hague in 1980:

> I wander through the great halls and every now and then, two corridors to the left, or two corridors to the right, I see Johnny Logan gliding past with the swarm in pursuit. I try several times to catch up, but it is futile. I meet no one I know, and despite my highly recognizable stripy blazer, my chocolate-brown straw boater, my yellow trousers, my yellow shirt and my sand-coloured beach shoes, nobody hails me as the guy whose song has just scooped the prize. Like an invisible man, I wander from room to room in a spaced-out trance.[7]

Emmelie de Forest, the 2013 winner, onstage in Malmö.
(Photo: Joanna Seels/Jason Howes)

---

[7] *On the Road... From Tara to Tiananmen Square by Way of Chuck Berry*, Shay Healy, O'Brien Press, 2005.

Niamh Kavanagh won in 1993 with what many regard as Ireland's best winning song, *In Your Eyes*. Could she have capitalised more on her success? Niamh replied:

> Yes, is the simple answer. I did what I could at the time. I made mistakes and so did other people, but I think that is true for lots of people in this industry.

She came back to the Contest with gusto in 2010, having spent many of the intervening years as a member of a cover band, 'The Illegal Eagles', with her husband, Paul Megahey. She was one of the most amiable artists I ever worked with. Even when she was demanding, she did it in a gentle way. Luck wasn't with her in Oslo, and though she came through the semi-final, a glut of ballads that year was one of the reasons she had to be content with a nineteenth place finish. She has no regrets, however:

> I have discovered over time that Eurovision is the gift that keeps on giving, because you are part of the history and the fans are so true to it, they always want to see you.

She recalls what Jimmy Walsh said to her, when he gave her his song, *In Your Eyes*:

Winners: Niamh Kavanagh and Johnny Logan in Oslo in 2010

'Eurovision is what you want to make of it,' and I can honestly say that I have rarely heard a truer word. From that day I have a huge respect for Eurovision in all its forms. I won't say that I live a Eurovision life, but I love to visit it and I am thankful for the gifts it gave me.

In 1994, 'the year *Riverdance* won', as Charlie McGettigan calls it, people in the green room were telling Paul Harrington and Charlie that they'd won while the voting was still going on – that their points couldn't be beaten. Charlie recalls the moment:

> I could see the guitar sitting over in the corner but I wasn't going to touch it until the final votes were in. You see, I was never good at maths.

Following their victory, he believed that as far as he was concerned, the fame would be a temporary thing.

> The extent of it was very quickly apparent when we played a gig a few weeks after the win in a place called Carrick Springs in County Cavan. It was a venue that held over 1000 people. We had 14 people at our gig. However, one of the 14 was a man called Gotfried Brinkman, an industrialist from Germany who invited us to play at his parties on several occasions.

'The Eurovision saved my life, work-wise,' says Linda Martin, looking back twenty-five years after her win in Malmö with Johnny Logan's song. She was working in a band, Chips, who knew their stuff, but she says, there was 'no light at the end of the tunnel'. As for Eurovision, she echoes Niamh Kavanagh's view: 'It's a gift that keeps on giving. I still get asked to do gigs in Europe.'

Going back to the ESC, as she did in 2012, to work with Jedward and RTÉ in Baku, was a good experience. For her, the best part was the can-do attitude of the producers, despite the number of countries involved in the shows:

Linda Martin watches the scoreboard in Malmö in 1992. Left is Kevin Linehan, Head of Delegation that year, right, Alan Pentony, a backing vocalist. Johnny Logan is standing behind. (© RTÉ Archives)

You remember when we said we'd love a fountain on the stage and we'd also like John and Edward to jump into it at the end of the song? They just said, 'Okay, bring it over!'

Linda Martin's positivity about Eurovision continues. She has always said, too, that a good song will always triumph over any voting pattern.

Eurovision has given great starts to artists that don't necessarily have a profile in this part of the continent. We forget there are such big territories out there – Russia, Germany... where people can sell so many CDs. We think we're the centre of everything, but we're not.

The victory of the Russian, Dima Bilan, in Belgrade in 2008 is evidence of this.

Bilan, an actor, singer, and songwriter, is a huge star in his native country and parts of Eastern Europe, yet he doesn't seem to have been as attractive to Western ears. He had of course come second in 2006, so had form. When he came back in 2008, armed with a small ice rink on the stage, graced by an Olympic medal-winning figure skater, Evgeni Plushenko, he won. In the act they also had the Hungarian violinist Edvin Marton, known as the 'violinist of the skaters', complete with Stradivarius. Along the Danube basin they were impressed, but less than one-third of his winning points came from the West. Six countries from 'old Europe' gave his song *Believe* no points at all – Denmark, Belgium, Sweden, the UK, San Marino and Switzerland. Ireland broke ranks and gave him seven.

Bilan arrived in Ireland that year, as part of the 'Winner's Tour', a short-lived initiative by the EBU to try to make the artist and song 'travel', and achieve something more from winning Eurovision than just one night of glory. (As it turned out, the digital era made this kind of physical presence approach virtually obsolete.) Michael Kealy was the person who had to 'mind' him in Dublin. He recalls that it was a lovely late May evening, so after the rehearsal for *The Late Late Show* he suggested it would be nice to walk the 500 metres or so to a local hostelry for something to eat. After about 100 metres he says, 'it was clear Dima didn't do walking'. After the fish and chips, Kealy decided to walk back and get his car for the star's return to the studios.

> Dima was a Diva. But he had a stunningly beautiful manager called Sasha Tityanko (I'll never forget that name!). But it was clear she regarded Ireland as close to the nadir of their winner's tour. After collecting Dima I was dispatched by her to buy a power lead for her Apple Mac. I did it willingly – she had that effect on men!

After all the ups and downs and the thrill of the whole thing, all the glamorous Eurovision singers realise sooner or later that age does creep up on you. Sandie Shaw, the barefoot 1967 winner, announced her retirement from music in 2013 at the age of sixty-six, as it happens, a year after Loreen from Sweden had won without wearing footwear onstage. And what of those feet that charmed Europe in the 1967 Contest? Shaw decided in 2007, after all the fame they'd brought her that they needed corrective surgery, the BBC reported in August that year. Though admitting the irony of saying at this stage of her life that they were 'ugly', she said that she 'always wanted beautiful feet'.

The members of Lordi might have found the twenty-year-old Sandie's limbs attractive had they been around the Contest in 1967. But their

Lordi's moment of victory, Athens, 2006

year was definitely 2006. Kjell Eckholm, Finland's Head of Delegation that year, says Finns had already given up on ever winning the Contest and thought 'we might as well send these monsters out to Europe so we'll give everybody something to talk about'.

May in Athens tends to be sweltering. And it's even hotter inside monster masks, but they had to be worn all the time – it was part of the Lordi act. No exceptions – not even it seems in the privacy of their Eurovision dressing room. 'They put on the plastic dresses at nine in the morning and took them off at eleven in the evening in a hot, hot Athens,' recalls Kjell Eckholm, 'but man, what a smell when they took them off!'

He recalls Lordi as a thoroughly professional act.

> Artists often get nervous and start complaining ... about the hotel ... or the food. Not these guys. Nothing was a problem.

He says it was because they had slogged it around Europe in a bus trying to make it. Eurovision's comforts were like heaven to them. Kjell says that the band had never even watched Eurovision on television. They were coming from a different musical space. They thought they'd have a go and the unexpected happened. He heard by an accidental leak that they had romped home in the semi-final, so he knew something big was on the cards. But eight years on, Lordi still hasn't repeated the success of *Hard Rock Hallelujah*, nearly ten years on. 'Albums, different producers, but they have struggled in vain to get that follow-up hit.'

Another colourful winner, Dana International, aka Sharon Cohen, who in her own way had changed the face of the Contest in 1998, was involved in one of Eurovision's famous incidents. She was appearing in Jerusalem in the 1999 Contest, hosted by Israel, but as she carried the heavy trophy to present it to Sweden's winner, Charlotte Nilsson, one of the composers of the winning Swedish song stepped on the long trail of her dress by accident and she fell over on stage – in front of the

Sertab Erener, the winner for Turkey with Every Way That I Can, *in Riga in 2003. The song was one of those to successfully combine pop with ethnic rhythms and motifs in the Contest during the last ten years.*

massive television audience, making it one of the most memorable moments in the history of the Contest.

Cohen campaigned for the moderate Israeli political party, Kadima, in 2009, before returning to the Contest in 2011. She didn't make it into the final that year, the first Eurovision returning winner not to do so. She left Düsseldorf in a huff the day after the semi-final. She had been staying in the same hotel as the Irish delegation. She had her pride, of course, but we just concluded she was a bad loser.

Celine Dion is a former winner who needs no introduction. Her brush with Eurovision, though it wasn't really her career springboard, produced its own drama in Dublin in 1988. The UK, with their singer Scott Fitzgerald, were denied a fifth victory, which would have brought them level with Luxembourg's winning tally, by a single point, when the last jury, Yugoslavia, delivered its result, giving nothing to the UK song. Dion, the nineteen-year-old native French-Canadian had come from nowhere to bring Switzerland victory with *Ne Partez Pas Sans Moi.* Liam Miller, Executive Producer that year, recalls that the UK delegation was 'fit to be tied'. They were furious with the Yugoslav jury, for starters, and angry that Dion seemed to have come from nowhere, and wasn't even from Switzerland.

At any rate, unlike Scott Fitzgerald, Celion Dion became a megastar during the 1990s, but her rise had only a small connection with her Eurovision win. Unlike *Waterloo,* her winning song didn't do well in the charts around Europe. Yet her eventual career fortune would rival the great Swedish quartet.

So, back to those folk with the platform shoes – the Abba question. When the ESC was celebrating fifty years with the Copenhagen show in 2005, and despite the fact that *Waterloo* in the run-up to the occasion was voted the 'second best Eurovision song of all time', nothing could persuade the four to do what could be called a 'lap of honour'.

In an interview with the *Sunday Telegraph* in 2008, at the time of the premiere of the *Mama Mia* movie, Björn and Benny confirmed that there was nothing that could entice them back on stage again. The rumour had always been that mega-money was on offer. Ulvaeus gave a considered view:

> We will never appear on stage again. There is simply no motivation to re-group. Money is not a factor and we would like people to remember us, as we were – young, exuberant, and full of energy and ambition.

He then turned to the world of rock 'n' roll for a useful metaphor:

> I remember Robert Plant saying that Led Zeppelin were a cover band now because they cover all their own stuff. I think that hit the nail on the head.

It had all started with making the most of their three minutes to shine in this pan-European event, the continent's biggest TV entertainment spectacle, the Eurovision show itself.

Chapter 4

The Shows, the Event, the Glitter

What is it that makes hundreds of fans stand around watching rehearsals in a cavernous stadium in the summer heat, while backing tracks boom, singers strut, lighting crews tweak equipment and delegations complain, enduring stop-starts and constant repetition? They come because they're addicted to the formbook. Who will crack? Will the thoroughbred fall at the first fence? Who is the dark horse? The sound thunders around a cavernous stadium as they discuss, text, tweet – and bet.

Diarmuid Furlong perhaps speaks for fans everywhere when he says:

> ... you also always get very patriotic at Eurovision, so no matter what you think of the Irish entry, you will always back the Irish team 100 per cent and then can be quite disappointed with the end result. Watching rehearsals is crucial.

So, to get a sense of the breadth and scale of the show, it's worth comparing and contrasting locations in the changing Eurovision story – the village of Millstreet in Ireland with a population of 1,500 people, and Moscow with its 11 million inhabitants.

In 1993, the village of Millstreet in County Cork in the southwest of Ireland had no restaurants, and a small railway station. But it did a have an arena called the Green Glens. It was the largest venue outside the capital and was used for equestrian events. It was on one occasion famously described by the BBC as a 'cowshed'.

The legend goes that Linda Martin hadn't even finished singing her reprise after winning the Contest in Malmö with Johnny Logan's song *Why Me?*, when the venue's owner, Noel C. Duggan, reprising the song's title, began his letter to RTÉ, asking basically, 'why not Millstreet for 1993?'

For all kinds of reasons, not all necessarily to do with the show itself, the national broadcaster bought into the idea. A local, roughly written verse by a Francis Duggan, sums up the folksiness of it all:

> Noel C Duggan the entrepreneur of Millstreet Town,
> The fellow who did dream of Worldwide renown,
> Did dream that the 1993 Eurovision Song Contest at his Green
>   Glens Complex would take place,
> No challenge for him seems too daunting to face.

> Noel C Duggan did dream and his dream did come true
> The man is a genius to give him his due,
> He brought The Eurovision Song Contest to the Town
>   of Millstreet,
> At his Green Glens Arena for glory Europe's best did compete.

The venue had no real advantage over the Royal Dublin Society's Simmonscourt Pavilion, used for the 1988 Contest, but there were 'local politics' in play and a 'why not' attitude by the broadcaster. So bulldozers had to come in to lower the arena's floor. Liam Miller, the Executive Producer that year, says the budget wasn't significantly higher than if they had stayed in Dublin. The hotels available in Killarney were only about thirty minutes away by bus. But it all took work. He recalls saying to his wife one morning as he was going down to Millstreet, that there was a problem that needed sorting out. He came home seven weeks later: 'You had to manage the politics of it day by day.'

When the producer of the show, Kevin Linehan, had got almost to the rehearsal stage, he and Miller discovered that Noel C. and local people had, as Miller says:

> ... turned the Green Glens Arena into a theme park. They put up fences and were charging entry. We then agreed that the money raised would go to a local community group.

We think of marketing and branding as a later phenomenon in entertainment TV, but Miller also recalls that RTÉ came under significant commercial pressure that year – from Philips – to adopt a form of telephone voting, and that the marketing company who made the approach in early 1993 'were not best pleased' when their advances were rebuffed. It was before new commercial thinking emerged at the EBU.

By total contrast, in the space of sixteen years, when the Contest came to Russia in 2009, it being that vast country's first win, it was inevitable that things were going to be big. It was becoming what has been described as a 'logistics competition', as the Reference Group or the EBU do not place limits on a host broadcaster's spend.

John Casey is an Irish-born production designer who was hired by Channel One, the Russian broadcaster producing the Contest in 2009. He recalled afterwards how he was flown first class from New York where he was working when his services were requested by Moscow. He asked what was the budget he had to work with. 'There are no limits,' he was told. He then said they must have an upper figure in mind, but the answer was repeated, 'there are no limits'. Russia went on to break all spending records for the Contest, clocking up over €30 million.

Below, some of the technical spec for the Moscow shows:

Stage Technical Equipment

- LED – 2,000 square metres
- Lights – 1,723 devices
- Metal truss length – about 3 kilometres
- Total cable length – over 120 kilometres

- Sound equipment total power – 150 kW

- Total power supply – 10 MW

- Total weight of the equipment and stage structures was 650 tons, including 150 tons of suspended equipment.

It was the largest Eurovision stage ever – Russia saw to that. The LED video wall was gigantic. Peter Canning from Dublin was assistant to the lighting director, Al Gurdon. As a lighting professional, he wasn't complaining about the scale. He found the huge budget was in most ways a credit to Russia. His caveat, though, is that it shouldn't always be about 'lighting by numbers', as he calls it:

> You'd hear people say, 'Oh can we have a thousand of these lights and forty kilometers of that cable' – the technology has got so big that it can be overpowering.

But, he maintains, the songs that win are the ones that visually stick out. 'Everyone remembers Iceland that year', he maintains, 'the fantastic glass ship moving behind the singer, Yohanna.' Canning was in Dublin in 2014 when he got texts from the arena in Copenhagen from a couple of crew members on the site, who had never heard of the 'bearded lady', Conchita Wurst, who was about to become very famous, but said that there were amazing graphics on the Austrian song: 'I think it was Louis Walsh who said once that music now was seventy per cent visual, only thirty per cent music.'

But technology can have its pitfalls. Estonia's representatives in Moscow were Urban Symphony. The song was called *Randajad.* The show's graphics team created a beautiful water scene, Canning recalls. The title, which translated as *The Nomads,* might have been a clue to their error, but it wasn't until someone checked a translation of the song's first lines that the penny dropped:

> In the desert heat, the sand
> Blows like ice-cold snow.

The Malmö Arena, venue for the 2013 Contest.
(Photo: Joanna Seels/Jason Howes)

A band called Lovebugs were the Swiss artists in that Moscow Contest. *The Highest Heights* was their song, so, not too surprisingly, the graphic people came up with a Swiss Alps theme. The band weren't impressed, stopped during their first rehearsal and one of them said, 'You make us look like a chocolate box!'

Graphics can sometimes be 'too' good, however. Jedward's design for Düsseldorf in 2011 was just that – for two reasons. Firstly, the design, created by a Dublin company, Tangerine, and masterminded by Caroline Downey, who was the twins' 'mentor', was so impressive that the multi-camera director wanted to feature it strongly, and in so doing had far too many wide shots in the song, at least in Ireland's view. The delegation made a last minute plea to get a few more close-ups of the twins, with some success. This is all part of the 'cut and thrust' of Eurovision participation. Looking back now, it still errs a little on the wide.

*Loreen, the Swedish winner in 2012, with
identical twin brothers from Dublin*

The second consequence of this piece of software was that a rule
was made for Azerbaijan the following year that all stage graphics were
to be generated by the shows' production team. The Jedward package
had been supplied complete. I was asked, as Head of Delegation, not to
reveal this to any other country, as the team had rejected several other
packages they considered inferior, and so didn't want a precedent set
by accepting Ireland's completed one.

There are certain items in the Eurovision production and staging
that are a given each year; for example, the number of rehearsals and
the pre-recorded clips between each country's song, called 'postcards'.

Countries' commentators talk over them, sometimes mocking them. They have varied in artistic quality. The 2010 postcards were based on an observation by the show's producer, Hasse Lindmo, of a natural phenomenon that was featuring on the Internet: wild birds, swallows and rooks, flying in artistic sweeping movements, as if coordinated. The basic synopsis of his postcard concept was a group of numerous little balls (the theme of the Norwegian ESC) forming the shape of each country. Then they move and form a screen where we can see a pre-recorded video of a little crowd gathering to support and cheer the act in a city of the country (usually the capital). The Norwegian idea was good, but required a lot of work by each country. I remember we in RTÉ had to arrange a 'flash mob', which we willingly did. We assembled about three to four hundred people in Meeting House Square in Dublin. But when it got to the Eurovision we, like the other countries who got involved, received just a few seconds on screen.

Every country tries to make their act stand out. The stage in Düsseldorf in 2012 wasn't as big as the Moscow one, but nevertheless, Sweden decided to take a bold – some might say cheeky – approach to make an impact. They dispensed altogether with the giant stage, the one that everyone else took for granted.

Lene, the winner for Germany in Oslo in 2010

Incident in Kiev, 2005. The Irish backing vocalists/dancers decided to illustrate their talent at a press conference, but the table gave way.

Their prop was *their own* stage, wheeled in and assembled following the preceding act.

Then, as Loreen performed, there were hardly any wide shots; the lighting was white and blue only, with no flashing images. It was the singer in low light, tossing her hair and singing her disco/trance song *Euphoria*. When she finished, we were 'returned' to the colourful stage. The Swedes, veteran ESC participants, its nobility perhaps, had pulled off a visual coup d'état. The result, with their combination of song, singer and staging, was a record: eighteen countries out of the forty-two participants awarded *Euphoria* twelve points.

If Russia in 2009 was the zenith of the gigantic spectacle, fortunately, for the Contest's viability, the following year's hosts, Norway, pulled back from the big spend and looked for a more creative, rather than quantity-led, solution to the staging of Eurovision.

It was fitting also, that when the stage and the props seemed to be getting bigger and bigger, along with the crews needed to maintain them (I remember watching welders at work between rehearsals on Ukraine's giant three wheel machine in Moscow), along came Lene from Germany in Oslo, 2010, wearing a simple 'high street' dress, with an old fashioned three backing vocalists combo beside her, no elaborate choreography, to triumph with *Satellite*. Norway's production and Lene's sparse act's success were perhaps, in different ways, role models of sustainability.

The venue and the act can be big or not so big, but in the end it's about the songs.

The finale in Copenhagen in 2014
(Photo courtesy Andres Putting, EBU)

Chapter 5

It's a Song Contest?

Thomas G:son, a 'serial' Eurovision songwriter, having entered nearly seventy songs in various countries' selection competitions, and one of the writers of the Swedish winner in 2012, *Euphoria*, made an interesting – and revealing – admission in a German newspaper in 2013, when commenting on the alleged plagiarism of his song: 'In general,' he said, 'pop songs are alike.'

Whether this is true or not, Dr. Aileen Dillane of the University of Limerick thinks the best thing about the Contest, while acknowledging the power of it as a spectacle, are the songs:

> They are so varied, encompassing so many genres, sounds, beats and grooves. We may joke that there's a formula – verse, chorus, middle eight, soaring half step key change to the climax, and so on, but in the end it proves very hard to fashion that winning song, to predict what will appeal to the audience in a given year.

Diarmuid Furlong believes that before televoting came into the equation, there was an idea of what a perfect Eurovision song might actually be:

> You either had the perfect 'Eurovision ballad' or the perfect 'Eurovision pop song' or what you thought might appeal to juries. However since televoting was introduced in 1997,

what appeals to people one year, may not necessarily work the following year.

Niall Mooney, who co-wrote Ireland's entries in 2009 and 2010, says he has tried to guess what the formula is on countless occasions, but believes most of the time it's the best combination of song, singer and staging.

> I would actually point to what The Netherlands did last year with The Common Linnets duo. Most people would advise against a country song but look at how well they did. It wasn't typical Eurovision, but it was a very good song performed really well with simple, effective staging. It came second but charted all over Europe.

Mickey Joe Harte on stage in Riga in 2003. He was the first artist chosen to represent Ireland by means of the TV talent show, You're a Star.

Where do great – winning – songs come from? From chance some of the time. Good fortune, too. Take the case of Ireland's winner in 1980, *What's Another Year?* Its writer, Shay Healy, describes being on a bus journey in Dublin and hearing someone say 'what's another year?' He told the story in his autobiography:

> Songwriters are weirdos. We spend our time hearing possible lines of songs in the things people say. I got off the bus, turned up my collar and put my head down into the cold December wind. The phrase had snagged my songwriter's brain and my creative juices began flowing:
>
> *I've been waiting such a long time*
> *Reaching out for you but you're not here…*[8]

When he finished writing it, Healy recorded a demo with some musician friends, who cut it as a 'nice medium-tempo country-ish ballad'. When the song was then selected for Ireland's National Song Contest, he turned to another friend, a man who later became world famous as the composer of *Riverdance*, Bill Whelan.

Whelan literally transformed the song. In an echo of another great musical event, the moment in 1978 when Gerry Rafferty asked Raphael Ravenscroft if he could play some sax on a song he was recording called *Baker Street*, creating a musical legend, Whelan engaged another horn player, Colin Tully, and the result, as Healy describes, 'lifted the song out of its marshmallowy, country lethargy, and made it into a sophisticated, ever-green, classy ballad'.

The writing and recording process isn't always as successful – or as apparently trouble-free. Originality, or alleged lack of it, can rear its head. The dreaded word is plagiarism.

In a much loved episode of *Father Ted*, Father Ted Crilly is on the brink of Eurovision fame when it's discovered he has 'borrowed' an earlier Norwegian song, so his effort ends in ignominy.

---

[8] *On the Road… From Tara to Tiananmen Square by Way of Chuck Berry,* Shay Healy, O'Brien Press, 2005.

In 2003, life imitated art, in a sense, when the EBU's Reference Group had to launch an inquiry after claims that Ireland's proposed entry, *We've Got the World*, written by Martin Brannigan and Keith Molloy and sung by Mickey Joe Harte, sounded suspiciously similar to the winning Danish entry in 2000, *Fly on the Wings of Love*.

The broadcaster and the singer had what might have seemed the unlikely backing

Thomas G:son, co-writer of Euphoria, *in Copenhagen, 2014 (Photo: Albin Olsson)*

of Jorgen Olsen, who performed and wrote *Fly on the Wings of Love*. Although the Danish singer-songwriter said there were similarities between the two songs, he added that he did not believe his work had been plagiarised. He appeared on an Irish radio programme, *Liveline*, where the presenter Joe Duffy played both choruses, repeatedly asking the Dane if he thought there was a similarity, something that seemed clear to many of the listeners.

In the end, the Reference Group saved embarrassment for Ireland by stating that the song didn't breach the Eurovision Song Contest rule that states a song mustn't have been 'previously released'. Kjell Eckholm, who was a member of the Reference Group then, and a person who has examined many plagiarism controversies, says:

> I would have been in a court case with *We've Got the World*. I would say it was a case of plagiarism.

He points to George Harrison and the *My Sweet Lord* and *He's So Fine* case. The court concluded that the earlier tune had been 'subcon-

*Linda Martin with backing singers,
Leanne Moore, left, and Claire O'Malley,
at the 'Welcome Party' in Baku in 2012*

sciously copied', because in 1963 the Beatles and the Chiffons had songs in the British chart at the same time, so it was highly possible that Harrison had heard *He's So Fine*.

The truth is that nearly every year the Eurovision has at least one plagiarism controversy. In 2001, the Swedish song, *Listen to Your Heartbeat*, was accused of plagiarising the Belgian entry for the 1996 Contest, *Liefde is een Kaartspel* (Love is a Card Game). The case was settled between the parties with the Swedish record company apparently paying a substantial sum to the Belgian writers.

In 2013, Cascada's entry for Germany, *Glorious,* was the subject of an investigation by the host broadcaster, Norddeutscher Rundfunk (NDR), following allegations that it was too similar to the 2012 winner, *Euphoria.* When *Bild* interviewed Thomas G:son and Peter Boström, the composers/producers of *Euphoria,* G:son was asked about going to court about the matter and said:

> We definitely feel honoured. It's not plagiarism to us, however. If you look at the composition in a waveform, you will see that 10,000 pop songs have similar courses.

It was later announced on 25 February 2013 by NDR that *Glorious* was cleared of plagiarism and would represent Germany at the Eurovision Song Contest in 2013.

Good company: Loreen, the Swedish winner in 2012, with Jedward, in Baku. The twins share an honour with the Swedish singer: Both were recipients of the Marcel Bezeçon Eurovision Commentators Artistic Award, John and Edward in 2011, Loreen the following year. Christer Bjorkman, who founded the Marcel Bezecon Awards and sang for Sweden in 1992, is a veteran of the Melodifestivalen, and produced the Eurovision shows in Malmö in 2013.

G:son, and writers like him, brings us to the huge phenomenon in the Eurovision in the last ten years: the trend of international co-writing, with often up to four writers taking credits. Allied to this is a very strong Swedish influence, the 'Swedish song factory' as the trend has been referred to. One RTÉ executive calls it 'the Swedish virus'. Countries as far apart geographically as Azerbaijan and Ireland have entered songs written, or part-written, by Swedish writers. It was a virtual epidemic. It produced the desired result for Azerbaijan in 2012. Their winner, *Running Scared*, sung by El and Nikki, was written by Stefan Örn and Sandra Bjurman from Sweden, working with Ian Farquerson from the UK. Örn and Bjurman were also authors of the song *Drip Drop,* which represented Azerbaijan in 2010, coming fifth.

Some fans found the formulaic sound of some of these songs 'written by committee' increasingly apparent, but not so the voters, it seems. Multi-writer penned songs triumphed in both 2013 and 2014, though only the first one involving Swedish composers. *Only Teardrops* and *Rise Like A Phoenix* were very different songs, but the phenomenon, driven partly by technology and the internet, looks set to continue.

What makes a Eurovision winning song? Some have suggested that there is a formula, but happily there isn't. Winners generally have factors in common, for example, the chorus standing out from the verse, giving the song an extra kick. Great choruses lift the song from the verses but are still connected musically. Think of *Waterloo* and *Hold Me Now.* A key change towards the end is a good idea, but not mandatory for success.

Maybe in the end the only formula is that there is no formula. For example, what do we remember about the 2014 winner, Conchita Wurst? Most viewers will remember the beard, perhaps the lighting design, definitely the voice, but not many will recall the song so easily.

Linda Martin puts her finger on a simple point about success and failure.

> If you watch a singer from, say Ukraine, regardless of whether the song itself is good, bad or indifferent, they come out onto that stage and they look the part, number one. They're camera aware, secondly. And then there are the energy levels – even if it's a ballad. I don't know what it is; I can only describe it as electricity.

And Linda knows. She was part of Ireland's glory years.

Chapter 6

Faded Glories: Ireland and the UK

When Queen Elizabeth II made her momentous visit to Ireland in 2011, and spoke eloquently about what both countries had in common, she might well have mentioned the Eurovision Song Contest, though she didn't. Most of us are aware of the musical connections that span the Irish Sea, but looking at the Eurovision, the United Kingdom and Ireland have known great rivalry but also share surprisingly similar experiences on the ESC stage.

Tim Moore captured a moment in that Britain and Ireland relationship, as his 'journey' to meet the recipients of 'nul points' was ending in the stadium in Kiev in 2005, and he waited in vain to hear a country give points to the UK entry, Javine, with *Touch My Fire*. Then he heard Dana Rosmary Scallon's voice, 'the gentle voice of Ireland's 1970 Eurovision winner, amplified to a godlike boom, blasts out around Kiev's Palace of Sport: "United Kingdom, eight points!"'[9]

To start with, the two islands have between them one-fifth of all Eurovision winners; both are in the 'elite' group of only six countries who have won five times or more; the *Royaume Uni* and *Irland* have exchanged points with each other almost every year; and they have occupied the bottom of the scoreboard together. Most dramatically, neither country has been a winner – nor even close to it – since televoting was

---

[9] *Nul Points*, Tim Moore, Vintage, 2006.

firmly established in 1998. So did these neighbours become dinosaurs of the Eurovision as its musical centre of gravity moved east?

Even before we consider the record seven victories, Ireland's performance between its debut year, 1965, and the first win in 1970 would be the envy of most countries: sixth, fifth, second, fourth, and seventh. Then along came Dana and *All Kinds of Everything* in 1970 – achieving victory and an international hit.

The Johnny Logan triumphs followed in 1980 and 1987. He then entered the record books in 1992 by following his two victories as a performer with the songwriter first place in Malmö, where Linda Martin performed *Why Me?*

That began the 'winning streak' of the 1990s: 1993, 1994, and 1996 followed. For the record, of course, the Norwegian act that won in 1995 was 'half Irish', the violinist in Secret Garden being Fionnuala Sherry. Then, in 1997, to cap it all, Ireland with Marc Roberts came second. But that was it.

'Old enemies': Brian Kennedy with two UK fans in Athens, 2006

In the last ten years, Ireland has come last twice in the Contest, had to sit out a year in 2002, and in the semi-final era has failed to qualify for the final on four occasions.

So where did it all go wrong since the glory days? How was it that the stellar performing nation and record holder became at best just an average achiever in the Contest? To find out, we must first analyse the seven victories.

Firstly, one person, Johnny Logan, is largely responsible for three of the seven. The songwriter Brendan Graham then penned two others. So these two men have their names on the majority of the victories.

Secondly, in those days, the odds were better. When Dana won in 1970 in Amsterdam, only twelve countries competed. All the other six victories were in a contest of twenty-four or twenty-five participants, rather than approximately forty in the present-day competition.

Thirdly, in the jury era, being entitled to sing in English was a definite advantage. Six out of the seven wins were when the EBU's national language rule was in force. Three out of the UK's five wins were also in these periods.

Fourthly, the Contest moved away from the slow song, with a static singer, a style that Ireland seemed to excel in. There's an echo here with France, as its glory years in Eurovision were achieved with *chansons* or ballads. Ireland's entries floundered, somewhat ironically, in the 'post-Riverdance', highly choreographed, era of Eurovision.

And, while giving the singers and writers their due, there was some luck involved along the way; at least two of the 1990s wins were 'against the run of play', the juries going for the more 'left field' Irish songs rather than the favourites. In the case of Oslo in 1996, it would be hard to imagine a televote, if it had been the method then of deciding the winner, not beating *The Voice*, a wistful number, when the ebullient Gina G from the UK and her subsequent hit *Ooh Aah…Just a Little Bit* was available?

A more subjective factor, but no less important, I believe, was the caliber of singer selected by both countries on the Irish Sea over the years. The UK sent Cliff Richard to Eurovision twice; he came second both times, only missing victory by a point on the second attempt in 1968 (caused, it has been alleged, by a fascist dictator's intervention). Cliff was young, charismatic and a great singer. And he was a star. So was Sandie Shaw in 1967. Katrina (of Katrina and the Waves) was an experienced singer when she took the trophy in 1997. Lulu had had chart success with *Shout* before she took first place in 1967 (though shared with three other songs) singing *Boom Bang-A-Bang*. The UK also has an impressive runner-up record, having come second fifteen times.

Ireland also sent seasoned pop artists in the 1960s and 70s. Dickie Rock, Colm C.T. Wilkinson (later world famous as Jean Valjean in *Les Misérables* and the lead role in *Phantom of the Opera* on Broadway), Sean Dunphy and the Swarbriggs were all experienced professionals, used to being on a stage. Add a consummate performer like Linda Martin, whose record was coming a close second in 1984 and then winning six years later, and it makes for an impressive list.

Englebert Humperdinck and Leanne Moore, You're a Star *winner in 2008, now a journalist and television presenter, and a backing vocalist with Jedward, in Baku, Azerbaijan in 2012.*

Compare all this to more recent years. The UK were represented by singers like Englebert Humperdinck and Bonnie Tyler, who in their heyday would surely have been real contenders, but were now performing with voices and images probably past their 'sell by date'. Englebert was seventy-six when he took to the stage in Azerbaijan in 2012. The result: twenty-fifth place with twelve points, which didn't really surprise anyone. *The Telegraph's* Neil McCormick described Tyler's effort a year later:

> She may be 61, and her song may be a by-the-numbers power ballad written by a team of American hacks, but she has that cheese-grater soul voice that can make even the most throwaway lyric sound like a matter of life and death.

But it was to no avail.

But when none other than Andrew Lloyd Webber was persuaded to get involved as the songwriter for 2009, he brought not only prestige and credibility but also a top five finish.

Ireland's performers since 2000 were mostly newcomers, enthusiastic but inexperienced. The courage and enthusiasm of singers like Donna and Joe McCaul in 2005, and Ryan Dolan in 2013, were no

Joe McCaul, centre, with his sister, Donna, wearing the 'famous' jacket, right with red beret. Joe has a great comedic sense and on the trip to Ukraine, liked to entertain with his toy balalaika and a version of My Lovely Horse.

Joe McCaul on stage, in Kiev

match for what the Eurovision demanded. Donna and her brother had been selected through the *You're a Star* talent show, and I remember her saying pointedly to me, after they'd missed qualifying in Kiev:

> We had a great achievement in winning a big competition at home, then before we get a chance to enjoy that, we're put into this massive show.

After the glory of the 1990s, Ireland's fortunes had reached a low when it had to sit out the Contest in 2002, after finishing twenty-first in 2001, such was the rule then. Kevin Linehan, then in charge of Ireland's Eurovision efforts, decided on a radical change of approach and hatched a plan with another producer, Larry Bass. A talent show, *You're a Star*, would be run over several weeks and the winning singer and song would be Ireland's Eurovision Song Contest entry. The plan had the positive result of bringing record audience figures for the ESC in 2003, when Mickey Joe Harte stormed to victory with his trademark prop, a green acoustic guitar. He came a creditable eleventh, so Ireland had a pass to the final in 2004. This selection method went downhill from there; twenty-third in 2004 and non-qualification in 2005. Donna and Joe McCaul had bravely faced a final of twenty-eight countries, with only ten to qualify – savage odds. Their fourteenth place wasn't good enough. I recall being with Joe when he did a radio interview the next morning in which he was asked why he thought the song hadn't qualified. He blamed 'bloc voting', though I advised him it mightn't have been the case. When the results of the semi-final were made public two days later, it turned out that he and his sister had received fifty-three points, the majority, twenty-nine, coming from countries in the so-called 'eastern bloc', among them Poland, Romania, Croatia and Hungary.

The Dustin act in Belgrade, Serbia, in 2008

There was another lesson for Ireland in recent years: don't mess with the Eurovision. Dustin was the democratic choice by Ireland in 2008, but with only twenty-two points, coming fifteenth out of nineteen countries in his semi-final, Dublin's foul-mouthed turkey failed to qualify. Whether it was the result of cynicism about the Contest, as many believed, but Dustin received almost half of the votes cast in the Irish selection show. There was considerable coverage of his win worldwide, but the novelty had well and truly worn off by May. Ireland was left with a poor vocal performance (though Dustin never claimed to be a singer), a slightly over-kitsch stage show and some fans in the audience booing. Michael Kealy, Irish Head of Delegation that year, recalls some consolation in jammed press conferences for Dustin, and some hilarious lines from the puppet. The UK learned a similar lesson with

Optimism: Dervish leaving Dublin airport for Finland, May 2007. They had pre-qualified, according to the rules then, because of Ireland's tenth place with Brian Kennedy in 2006. Front row; John Waters, Cathy Jordan and Tommy Moran.

Scooch and their 'airline steward kitch' routine in Helsinki in 2007, coming twenty-second.

And another lesson: don't preach at Eurovision. John Waters and Tommy Moran had written the song, *They Can't Stop the Spring,* for Ireland in 2007, celebrating political change in Eastern Europe. Whether it was the band's performance, indifference at the song's sentiment, or not wanting to be reminded of their recent past, the same East gave Dervish and the song no points, apart from five from Albania, the only score on the night.

Like the UK, which many would regard as the home of

Dervish onstage

*Advice: Johnny Logan talks to members of
Dervish in Helsinki in 2007*

Another endearing, but probably obscene, suggestion from Dustin? Dustin's alter ego, Johnny Morrison, hidden in the converted supermarket trolley for the performances, is a well-known practical joker. One gag was to borrow a mobile phone and then send a suggestive text to someone in the owner's contacts.

pop, Ireland can boast its share of star quality singers; it's just that the Eurovision isn't for them. This is partly due to the image of the Contest and partly because of the risk in competing and failing. When Ireland did send 'happening' acts, Brian Kennedy in 2006 and Jedward in 2011, the country was back in the top ten.

Media commentators in Ireland often wonder why we can't get back to 'winning ways', forgetting that the Contest has moved on in so many ways: musical taste has evolved, other countries invest more in their participation and the Contest has more status in many of these countries. Crucially, there are now often forty or more countries participating – all looking for a good result. As I argue elsewhere in this book, there's no discrimination

against the two 'veterans' on the western edge of the continent – no bias 'built into' the Eurovision, as some allege.

So expectations in this part of Europe have to be realistic. If we look at the example of a football competition, the UEFA European Championship, neither the UK or Ireland has won since the competition's inception in 1960. Diarmuid Furlong, President of the Irish branch of OGAE, says he gets annoyed when newspapers in Ireland are up in arms about the Irish result, calling for our withdrawal from the Contest because of 'all the eastern bloc voting':

> Translating it to sport, Ireland has made it to the quarter-finals of the World Cup on just one occasion, yet we would never call for the scrapping of our soccer team.

Niall Mooney, who co-wrote two Irish entries, in 2009 and 2010, and an accountant by profession, puts it in terms of figures:

> If you take it there are about forty countries regularly competing, that means that, on average, each country should have a top ten finish roughly every four years.

The truth is that both Ireland and the UK are short of even this level of achievement at present.

Could Ireland or the UK win the Eurovision Song Contest again? Of course they could. It might be that a big star may step up to the plate, or could it be a new voice suddenly appearing. In selecting Molly Sterling and *Playing with Numbers* in February 2015, the Irish televoters put their faith in modernity. Hope springs eternal.

Molly Sterling performing in the University Concert Hall, Limerick, at the final of the All Ireland Schools Talent Search, March 2014.
(Photo: Robbie McNabb)

Chapter 7

The Costs – and Who Pays?

L et's get the conspiracy theories out of the way first. There have always been rumours that some countries deliberately send songs that don't stand a chance of winning. Yet there isn't a shred of evidence for this. And what country would willingly abandon their pride just to avoid a huge cost?

And the costs are high. A Eurovision Song Contest hasn't come in under €20 million since Serbia hosted in 2008, and the broadcaster that year had to deal with the addition of a second semi-final for the first time.

The funding model is that all countries pay an affiliation fee, calculated using a formula based on their size, economy and host broadcaster's share of television viewing. A country like Ireland would contribute about €70,000, the UK a multiple of that. The total raised is in the region of €5 million. Less than that amount is available to the broadcaster staging the competition, as the EBU make deductions for their central costs and the supervision of the event. So generally not more than €3.5 million is available to the country staging the show. Ticket sales also contribute, in recent years between €1 million and €2 million. Sponsorship can provide some more funding, depending on a country's broadcasting code. Most of the ESC's international sponsorship money, the revenue from brands like Schwarzkopf and Raiffeisen

Bank, goes back to the broadcasters' coffers, as they are the ones taking the sponsorship 'bumpers' or 'stings' at their commercial breaks. The Helsinki ESC's balance sheet broke down as follows:

Income	Costs
EBU – €3.3 million	Show –€2.0 million
State subsidy – €4.0 million	TV production – €4.8 million
Tickets – €3.7 million	Event – €5.6 million
Other income – €1.4 million	
Total – €12.4 million	**Total – €12.4 million**

Local sponsors can be a revenue generator sometimes, but generally well over half of the host broadcaster's costs are paid for by the broadcaster itself, the city, or the government. Televoting is not the source or revenue that many believe it is: Firstly, only about one in ten viewers vote; secondly, in some countries the tariff is quite low; thirdly, the telecom companies and VAT takes their cut. And the remaining revenue doesn't go to the host broadcaster, but is, not surprisingly, given back to the broadcasters in whose country it was generated.

A *Guardian* writer, Jonathan Moles, in 2010 described the Eurovision as an 'annual test of new television and satellite technology dressed up as a music competition'. Yet it's this 'state of the art' approach that has kept the Contest relevant to television viewers.

Not only has a state-of-the-art stage to be provided, with kilometres of cable and thousands of lights, but also backstage facilities and security. Accreditation badges are a big cost, with over a dozen categories; coloured laminates are required for the several thousand participants and fans. In the audio department alone, in-ear monitoring has to be provided for almost 300 performers; that means an earpiece and power pack. The settings have to be adjusted and made ready for each rehearsal and performance. Because the shows are 'rehearsed to

A detail of Eurovision hosting: A young people's choir welcomed visitors to the Heads of Delegation meeting in Oslo, with a version of Sting's song Fragile, *in March 2010.*

within an inch of their lives' as one singer said, performers have to be corralled backstage and moved with military precision closer to the stage, as each of the other acts performs. Large stage crews have to practice the movement of often very large props on and off the stage in the thirty seconds that the 'postcards' allow.

The Düsseldorf ESC brought an unexpected cost for delegations. The city's hotels got together and agreed a 'minimum stay' rule for the Contest period across the city. Countries were obliged to pay for rooms that they weren't going to use. All hell broke loose with the participating broadcasters. NDR, the host broadcasters, did what they could to get something of a compromise eventually. It was market forces – greed – asserting themselves. It was just another Eurovision headache.

The EBU and Reference Group keep an eye on a host country's preparations. Sometimes with a new broadcaster, particularly if it isn't from the West, there's more scrutiny. The EBU always feared the consequences of a win by a country with less developed broadcasting know-how. The host country and city are also a concern for the marketing company, TEAM, as they have no choice as to where their campaign might be based each year. TEAM believe a big country isn't always desirable, either. A French or UK win, given their size and the ESC's weaker image there, mightn't be good for the Eurovision brand.

Yet the larger Western countries have a great privilege – they get a pass to the Eurovision final. There's no risk of semi-final humiliation for the UK, Germany, Spain, France or (the returning) Italy. This privilege's origins were in 1996 when, under the pre-selection rule at the time, Germany failed to quality. The EBU didn't want to lose a market that size. 'The Big 4' idea was born in 2000.

In the Reference Group, and the EBU in general, any idea that this might be changed was a non-starter. To the TEAM marketing colleagues, who were non-voting attendees, to suggest such a thing was heresy. So why did Russia, or Ukraine, with their huge populations, not object and look for the same arrangement? So far, these countries seem content to remain assessed differently by the EBU, pay less money and take their chances in the semi-finals. Italy's automatic admission to the club when they returned to the Eurovision in 2009 raised eyebrows, but that was all. For those representing small countries, an uneasy item in Reference Group meetings was the section that gave a special audience to the representatives of those countries every year.

Given the (publicly unstated) fear in the EBU of a Moldovan or Albanian win, it was ironic that an organisational controversy for the Eurovision happened in one of its most developed participants – Denmark. Who would have thought that a Contest staged in Copenhagen would be anything other than trouble-free? This was not to be in 2014.

Since the event in May that year, there's been a lot of bad publicity, mainly because of a massive cost overrun, though not for the shows themselves.

As background, these were some of the boasts that Danmarks Radio (DR) were able to make in the press kit for the commentators:

- Interactive LED stage floor (touch activated) never seen on TV before

- The cube surrounding the floor is covered with a transparent material that with the touch of a button becomes matte for content projection. The cube is manufactured from 40 tons of steel and is 20 meters tall.

Taxpayers in the Copenhagen area have to pick up the tab – and that hasn't made the show and the people behind it popular. The ESC

*Kjell Eckholm, left, Finnish Head of Delegation for several years and
veteran member of the Reference Group. On the right is Ferdinand Von Strantz,
an executive in TEAM Marketing, who has played a significant
role in the Eurovision since 2004.*

Jedward in Baku, Azerbaijan in 2012. They had returned to Eurovision with Waterline. In semi-final one they came sixth, with ninety-two points (fourth in the televote). In the final, however, they ended the voting in nineteenth place – tenth in the televote but twenty-fifth with the juries.

in Denmark has been referred to as 'The Big Eurovision Scandal' in the press. The venue for the shows was a dilapidated shipyard building on a small island in Copenhagen harbour, without infrastructure. Buildings had to be renovated and modified and new roads made to access the venue – and these costs overran budgets massively. The budget for all this was 34,600,000 DKK (€4.5 million) and the bill ended up 112,000,000 DKK (€15 million).

The Chairman of the Board, the CEO and one of the directors of the tourist organisation, Wonderful Copenhagen, have all been fired since. And it's not over yet, as DR is being investigated by government auditors because of contracts it made.

So winning can be a liability. Broadcasters fear it. Alarm went through RTÉ in 2011 when Jedward became favourites in Düsseldorf. When I left RTÉ in 2012 the Director General, Noel Curran, sent me a video message: 'I really appreciate your success in not winning the Eurovision!'

Russia delivered spectacular shows, at a massive cost. It may never be matched. This is how it broke down, with the shortfall clear:

Costs

Number	Items	Euro
1	Olympic Arena rent	2,080,000
2	ESC press center	1,279,000
3	Stage production	13,487,000
4	TV shooting	6,578,000
5	Olympic Arena organization and logistics support	6,072,000
6	Catering	753,000
7	Hotel accomodation and transport	351,000
8	Accreditation system	514,000
9	Sponsor areas	803,000
10	Green Room	714,000
11	Euroclub	2,411,000
12	Casualty insurance	15,000
13	Souvenirs and printed goods	342,000
	Total	**35,397,000**

Income

Number	Items	Euro
1	Income from EBU (participants' fees – 5,270 thousand CHF)	3,485,000
2	Income from international sponsors (EBU ~ 1,050 thousand CHF)	694,000
3	Income from national sponsors	1,917,000
4	Income from direct advertising in ESC 2009 broadcasting	117,000
5	Income from ticket sales (less agent's fees)	2,475,000
	Total	**8,959,000**

Value for money is crucial for most broadcasters nowadays. With the Eurovision Song Contest they get over seven hours of high quality television entertainment at a very competitive cost per hour. That's the unavoidable economic logic that, perhaps as much as any other reason, guarantees the competition's future.

But when money issues are dealt with, politics can suddenly rear its head.

Chapter 8

Politics Misses the Beat

Although it's TV entertainment, Eurovision doesn't exist in a political vacuum. Its interaction with the world's political realities is an essential – and fascinating – part of its recent and not so recent history.

In 2004, intrigue came to the Contest from the southeastern Mediterranean. The Lebanese broadcaster Télé Liban reached an agreement with the EBU and Lebanon was put on the official list of participants for the upcoming Kiev Contest. They had their song chosen, *Quand Tout S'Enfuit* ('When Everything Disappears'), sung by Aline Lahoud. But there was to be trouble ahead – making the song's title ironic. The rules of the Contest are clear: each country must broadcast the entire Contest. This is not an issue for most countries of course. But for this middle eastern country it was.

In Lebanon the authorities knew they'd have a problem showing the Israeli entry. But they kept going and a kind of cat-and-mouse game followed. Firstly, in March 2005, it was noticed that the official Lebanese Eurovision Song Contest website did not list Israel as a participant. After the EBU took up the issue with Télé Liban, the site removed the list of participants and replaced the page with a link to www.Eurovision.tv, the official Eurovision website. So the participation seemed to be back on track. At this stage the Lebanese broadcaster had paid their participation fee and the December deadline had passed whereby a country can withdraw without facing a penalty.

Perhaps sensing the possibility of embarrassment in Kiev during the Contest, the EBU then asked Télé-Liban for an assurance that they would broadcast the entire Contest, including the Israeli entry, without interruption. Télé Liban could not guarantee that request, so on 18 March 2005 it announced its withdrawal from the Contest, saying that 'it is not permitted to broadcast the performance of the Israeli participant, thereby breaching the rules of the Eurovision Song Contest 2005'. So they 'lost their deposit' and were further sanctioned by being disqualified for three years. There was talk of a Lebanese entry in 2009, but nothing came of it. And at that time, early 2005, there were bigger problems for the EBU with the Ukraine Contest.

Eurovision 'postcards', those video clips between songs, can generate unexpected trouble. They did just that in Moscow in 2009. Viewers might recall a lighter moment to the particular episode when the Armenian spokesperson read that country's results holding a clipboard with a picture of a statue. But this was no ordinary statue. The story had begun after the first semi-final, when representatives for Azerbaijan complained to the EBU that the video postcard before the Armenian song had contained a shot of this statue located in the Nagorno-Karabakh region, which Azerbaijan considers part of their territory. As a result of the complaint, the statue shot was cut out for the finals. However, Armenia weren't happy with this so they retaliated during the results presentation by both having the monument displayed on a video screen in the background, and featuring it on their presenter Sirusho's clipboard, in order to emphasise the point. Looking back now, former Executive Supervisor Svante Stockselius doesn't want to apportion blame:

> I think both are to blame. There is a very infected situation between these two countries but I don't think this special controversy was so serious.'

Diana Mnatsakanyan says Armenia wanted to make their point about the statue, while abiding by the Contest rules:

> The monument is depicting one of the most important values of Armenians – the family – sacred unity of a man and a woman, that stay shoulder to shoulder throughout the years, under the sun, in the wind, hit by the rain or snow, but firm as the mountains. There should be no controversy on this value as this is the way we are all brought up.

There were also allegations that during the show's broadcast in Azerbaijan no number had been shown for the public to call and vote for Armenia's entry. Somebody in the TV station in Baku had apparently made sure of this. Representatives denied these allegations by showing a video that showed an un-tampered signal during the Armenian performance. However, a subsequent EBU investigation found that Ictimai TV, the Azerbaijani broadcaster, had not only blurred out the voting details for Armenia's entry but also distorted the TV signal when the Armenian contestants were performing on stage. They were fined a substantial amount. Azerbaijan was also threatened with exclusions if further infringements of the Eurovision Song Contest rules took place.

There was a somewhat darker side to the affair later. In August 2009, a number of Azeri citizens who had voted for Armenia's entry during the 2009 Contest were summoned for questioning at the Ministry of Security in Baku, during which they were evidently accused of being 'unpatriotic' and 'a potential security threat'. This incident initiated another EBU investigation and discussion by the Reference Group that resulted in a change to the Eurovision rules to allow a country's participating broadcaster to be liable 'for any disclosure of information which could be used to identify voters'.

Azerbaijan then continued their efforts in the more peaceful task of trying to win the Contest, succeeding on their fourth attempt in 2011, hosting the Eurovision in lavish style – but in some controversy – the following year. There was talk of a boycott at one stage, because of the nature of the Azeri administration. Then there was relief all round when the respected Human Rights Watch said participation was preferable to a boycott.

During the Contest in Azerbaijan in 2012, that year's winner, Loreen, was the only artist to meet local human rights activists. She was quoted as saying, 'human rights are being violated in Azerbaijan every day, one should not be silent about such things'. Loreen, whose full name is Lorine Zineb Nora Talhaoui, born in Sweden of Moroccan-Berber roots, is now an ambassador for the Swedish Committee for Afghanistan, promoting development work there.

There is continuing unfinished territorial business in Europe. I was reminded of this during a discussion in the Reference Group in 2007. The country with a tongue twister of a name, the Former Yugoslav Republic of Macedonia, known as FYR Macedonia, was making another request to have the FYR officially dropped from their official Eurovision name. It seemed to me a reasonable request. The Greek member of the group, Fotini Yannoulatou, the Executive Producer of the Athens Contest in 2006, and not known for being easily angered, suddenly burst into a rage:

> Macedonia is part of Greece! They can't call themselves Macedonia. You should understand this.

Words and even letters can be important in these disputes; when the Contest was held in Athens in 2006, the host broadcaster, ERT, had insisted on not using the acronym, preferring to spell out the issue with the full wording, 'Former Yugoslav Republic of'. The name 'FYR Macedonia' sounded too close to 'Macedonia'.

Semantics – words and their meaning – were involved in another Reference Group debate in 2009, and this time the Georgian entry was involved. Georgia had decided in 2008 that they would not enter the Contest because of Russia's military intervention in South Ossetia. The decision was later reversed, partly, it seems, because of Georgia's win in the Junior Eurovision, the EBU's other annual song contest in December. So they were back in for the Moscow Contest – but there was a sting in the tail when their entry was decided on and submitted to the EBU in March. It was titled, *We Don't Wanna Put In,* a dance number by a band, Stefane and 3G. The title appeared innocuous until the words 'put' and 'in' are joined and a capital 'P' substituted. The chorus went:

We don't wanna put in
The negative move
It's killin' the groove.

The Russian broadcaster, Channel 1, which was hosting the Contest (extravagantly as it turned out), made a strong complaint, wondering why their prime minister should be maligned like this. In the Reference Group there were two views: one, that this was a clever, harmless jibe by Georgia; the other, that it both broke the rules about 'political songs' and was gratuitously insulting to the host nation. There were two Reference Group conference calls on the subject. It was clear to the members that Geneva didn't want any boats rocked on this thorny subject. The Russian member of the group, Yuri Aksyuta, also the Executive Producer of that year's Contest, was emphatic that the Georgian song was out of order. During the second discussion the Slovenian representative, Misa Molk, turned to the only native English speaker in the group, myself, after I suggested leniency towards Georgia, with a pertinent question: 'Have you ever heard people use the phrase, "want to put in"?' My answer was of course 'no', and that more or less ended the discussion. The agreed decision was to request that the song be altered. A serious diplomatic row had been averted.

On March 11, the Georgian broadcaster GPB announced that it would not change the lyrics of the song, or the song itself, claiming there were no political connotations within its lyrics, and perceiving the EBU's rejection of the song as political pressure from Russia. The country therefore withdrew from the Contest.

The Guardian's Moscow correspondent, Tim Jonze, saw a lighter side when he reported that it wasn't the first time Georgia has used disco music –unsuccessfully – in conflicts over its rebel region:

In 2007 authorities organized a concert by disco legends Boney
M – known for 1970s hits like *Rasputin* and *Daddy Cool* – in
South Ossetia to promote Tbilisi's efforts to regain control of
the region. It lost control of the entire territory a year later.

Then there are Eurovision controversies that don't get much trac-
tion. In 2008 a Spanish TV documentary alleged that the dictator Franco had influenced juries in several countries to get a win. Spain had
been getting single digit points in the preceding years. Suddenly, in
1968, they ended up with twenty-nine points with *La La La*, sung by
Massiel, one more than Cliff Richard with *Congratulations*.

The allegation caused a stir in Spain, as it implied that its only win
in the ESC's history was achieved by cheating. The story was never
convincingly substantiated, not even enough for the EBU to have an
investigation. I recall the Reference Group members' attitude to the issue as 'so what?' For the Spanish representative in the group, Federico
Llano, it was an unwelcome reminder of darker days in his country,

The author (left) with Federico Llano, Head of Delegation for Spain, a former
Reference Group member and currently a member of the EBU's TV Committee.

when interfering with a song contest would have been perhaps only one of the regime's minor crimes. Llano reflects:

> Who knows what really happened? It is sad for us to reflect that the only time Spain won (besides the four way tie in 1969) it could have been unfair. But no one has sought to find those who may have been guilty of accepting the bribery.'

Phil Coulter, the co-writer of *Congratulations* with a Scotsman, Bill Martin, doesn't lose much sleep over the *La La La* issue. On RTÉ Radio in 2013 he said the song owed a little to Lennon-McCartney's *With a Little Help from My Friends*, humming both to re-enforce his swipe: '*La La La* rocketed into obscurity', he quipped. His song, however, he said became the 'anthem of celebration' ever after. And he can say he had the honour of crossing legal swords with a Beatle, after George Harrison used the tune un-credited on his *All Things Must Pass* album.

But, apart from *Congratulations* and *Volare*, sung by the Italian Dominico Modugno, which, though it came third in 1958, went on to be one of the ESC's all-time most popular songs, generally the winner

Phil Coulter in Riga, Latvia, in 2003

is the one that 'takes it all' – or whatever fame is available – from the Eurovision Song Contest.

The year 2014 brought another small controversy from Georgia, a kind of throw-back to the Soviet era. The country's jury votes in the Grand Final were all declared invalid by the EBU, because for some reason all the jury members had voted exactly the same way, from their three point up to twelve points scores. According to EBU, this was a statistical impossibility. So only Georgia's televoting result was used for the distribution of the Georgian points in the final.

Flags and emblems will always bring headaches for Eurovision Song Contest producers. Take Norway in 2010, where use was made of national flags in the postcards. Some countries' actual geographical shapes, such as those for Serbia, Israel, Armenia and Azerbaijan, weren't completely shown, due to very real territorial or border disputes in those regions.

Fans in the Eurovision arena can show they care about things other than flags and whose song is better. In Copenhagen in 2014, Russia's act, the Tolmachevy Sisters, were booed by the audience during the semi-final, when they qualified into the final, and during the final itself, and when the Russian spokesperson was delivering their top-three votes. The booing was also heard when countries awarded Russia votes, which included Armenia and Belarus. The audience, it seems, was both expressing their feelings about Russia's actions in Ukraine and probably its new 'gay propaganda' law. The BBC's Graham Norton referred to this, and perhaps spoke for millions when he said:

> I feel so sorry for those two girls, they're only seventeen. It's unfortunate they're being subjected to it – but we totally understand it.

Some people online have recently called for Israel to be expelled because of the loss of life in 2014 in Gaza. But the counter-argument is that if a country's admission to a song contest was based on their political culture, or their international policies, where would it end? Russia, Belarus, Azerbaijan would certainly have to be looked at. And what

Jedward in Baku, Azerbaijan in 2012

would be the criteria for exclusion? Perhaps the audience expressing their protest, as in Copenhagen, is the best way.

The issue certainly provides more food for thought for the men and women behind the scenes, the people who guide Eurovision.

Jedward, drying off after a rehearsal in the fountain, outside the Crystal Hall in Baku. On the right is Clive Jackson, who designed and built the water feature for RTÉ, the idea having been suggested by that year's choreographer, Stuart O'Connor. Jackson had to travel to Baku ahead of the Contest to test it, and then maintain it throughout the rehearsals and shows. Several of us got involved in a late evening effort to clear an airlock after a failure at one of the rehearsals.

Chapter 9

Scenes from the Eurovision 'Backroom'

The Song Contest is the European Broadcasting Union's 'jewel' and great care is taken about how it's run. There have been important contributions to this task over the years, so here are some of the behind-the-scenes players and what they do.

The ESC final had started very smoothly in Oslo on 29 May 2010. The Spanish act was onstage, but something was wrong – there was an uninvited additional person in the act. An audience member, Jaume Marquet Cot, also known as Jimmy Jump, had joined Daniel Diges, uninvited, as he sang *Algo Pequenito*. The man ran off when security appeared, but the Spanish delegation was irate because the incident had taken from their performance – and their chances. They demanded they be given a reprise. The Contest's Executive Supervisor had a call to make.

But the fifty-something-year-old Swede, Svante Stockselius, didn't make a hasty decision. What would the other countries say if he granted the demands of Spain? So he thought laterally: he waited to see how the televote might pan out – were Spain contenders? Digame, the company that runs the vote, confirmed Daniel Diges and Spain were not in contention. So Stockselius knew he could accede to the request without incurring the wrath of the aggrieved Spanish, one of the Contest's 'big' countries. It was another decision made. Since 2003, the work of this quiet spoken, cool-headed man has made a most significant contribution to the Eurovision Song Contest.

I remember the first time we came across Svante in Ireland. It was in the aftermath of the bad result in the 2004 Contest in Istanbul. The Irish song had ended up in second to last place. Callers to the *Liveline* radio programme were furious and frustrated – and Eastern 'neighbour voting' was mostly to blame, as usual.

So into the cauldron of rage came Svante on the line from Sweden. He seemed to decide to take it head on and said that countries were actually entitled to vote for their neighbours if they wished – it was a free vote. It was a brave decision, given the atmosphere where people were looking for someone or something to blame. The listeners didn't seem to like his argument. But, as I discovered later, he had a point, and the self-confidence and authority to make it.

Stig Svante Stockselius was born in 1955 and grew up in Ockelbo, a small town in central Sweden. He started his career as a journalist, before ending up as head of the Entertainment division of the Swedish public service television company, Sveriges Television (SVT) in the late 1990s. He was involved in a major revamp of the Swedish ESC qualification competition, Melodifestivalen, in 2002, introducing four semi-finals and a 'second chance' round preceding the finals.

In 2003, the EBU appointed him ESC Executive Supervisor, succeeding Sarah Yuen, who had been in charge for the Riga Contest that year. He and the elected body, the Reference Group, set about making some changes.

Branding was their first step. A new generic logo was introduced in the run-up to Svante's first Contest at the helm, in Istanbul. It featured the heart-shaped flag in the center, thereafter changed each year. But the big change that year was the introduction of a semi-final. It was the latest solution for dealing with the influx of new countries to the competition. A record thirty-six had agreed to participate in Istanbul, including debuts from Albania, Andorra, Belarus, and Serbia and Montenegro. The previous solution for dealing with increased num-

*Svante Stockselius, in his customary position at the shows,
monitoring the voting*

ber of participants was that countries at the bottom of the scoreboard
in a particular year had to 'sit out' the next year's Contest. The new
semi-final plan involved a 'free pass' for the first ten countries from
the previous Contest; the 'Big Four' were guaranteed a place in the
final; then ten countries would qualify from the semi-final, making a
total for the final of twenty-four participants. This format remained in
place until 2008, when Serbia bravely agreed to take on the production
of two semi-finals.

All was going well in the semi, when a little glitch emerged during the counting of votes by Digame, the German company that have
run the televote for the EBU since that year. They discovered problems
with their calculation software, and there was a problem with text message voting in Croatia. When the votes were counted, results showed
that Croatia had awarded itself four points, which is of course against
the Contest's rules. An EBU statement said there had been technical
problems with the Croatian mobile service provider, who neglected
to delete the illegal votes from the results. Consequently, some votes
were not counted in the results announced at the end of the broadcast

of the semi-final. When the scores were corrected to include these additional votes, they were found – fortunately – not to have affected which countries qualified. The extent of the problem was not revealed publicly at the time. Svante recalls it now:

> For a couple of minutes I thought I had to go and inform some celebrating delegations that they did not make it to the final after all. Now this didn't happen, fortunately, and we learned a lot from these first mistakes.

There was another, smaller change. It was also the first year that the scores were only re-read by the hosts in one language. Before 2004 every point was repeated in French and English, but due to having thirty-six countries voting, and even more in years to come, in 2004 to save time the hosts only re-read each score in one language.

The year 2004 was also notable for another small detail: it was the first year that Turkey voted for Cyprus and the second year in a row that Cyprus voted for Turkey. Nevertheless, in a move that angered some Cypriots, when the country presented its votes, no map of the island was shown (all other presenters were preceded with their country being highlighted on a map). This was due to Turkey's claim that the northern half of the island is an independent republic, a claim that's not recognised anywhere else. It seems TNT decided not to show the map because it would have only highlighted the southern portion of the island, and thus angered the international community.

Svante is quiet spoken, but capable of assessing an issue with great clarity and acting with firmness. Most people could see why he had been trusted in different roles throughout his career. He became highly respected in the ESC world and, to some extent, feared. He could command a room full of delegations that often had complaints to make – about hotels or accreditation or the multi-cam director's work – but his put-downs of people and quick answers to questions with his precise English were legendary. He became a stern 'father figure'. Stockselius recalls modestly:

In this position you must be a successful diplomat. You need to listen, be clear, but also sometimes use a strong voice. I am proud of the respect I gave, and was given, by all delegations during my years.

The question would often be heard in ESC circles, 'What would Svante think of...?' Flattering to him, that question was still asked long after his departure. Diana Mnatsakanyan was 23 when she became Head of Delegation for Armenia. Determined, as she says, to 'examine the spinal cord of the ESC', she learnt a most important thing from Stockselius:

Whenever everything seems to be perfect, then something is definitely wrong. So there should be no time to lean back and relax after success, since success should be re-earned once again through an essential change.

Diana Mnatsakanyan, Head of Delegation for Armenia in the period between 2006 and 2010

The Executive Supervisor's job is to ensure that the Contest – the show and the event around it – happens smoothly each year, by close cooperation with the host broadcaster. He or she also has to report to EBU Headquarters in Geneva and to the Reference Group, of which he or she is a member, in the run-up to each Contest.

One of the Geneva EBU officials very involved in the Contest was a Dane, Bjørn Erichsen. He had been the boss of DR when they hosted the largest show up until then, in the 40,000 seat Parken Stadium in 2001. He could be outspoken and readily gave opinions. In March 2003, as Latvia prepared to do the Eurovision honours, the Danish newspaper *BT* published an article based on accusations that the EBU's Television Director, Bjørn Erichsen, made a reference to LTV, the Latvian host broadcaster that year, suffering from 'organisational chaos' which could result in the removal of Latvia's hosting duties since they were running behind schedule. The general director of LTV, Uldis-Ivars Grava, replied, saying:

> A few weeks ago, the EBU's legal director, Werner Rumphorst, was in Riga, and I spent an entire day with him and with the former general director of the Danish broadcaster DR (Danmarks Radio), Bjørn Erichsen. We talked about co-operation and about programme exchanges, and neither of them said a single word that would indicate any doubts, lack of trust or accusation.

Erichsen got involved in discussions in 2008 with the UK film production company, Working Title, in a plan to make a Eurovision movie, on the lines of their hits *Notting Hill* and *Love Actually*. Nothing eventually became of the plan, though a treatment was presented to the Reference Group.

In his championing the ESC's reputation, Erichsen decided in 2009 to take on Terry Wogan. He said the BBC man's commentary undermined the Contest's reputation. He accused the BBC and the British public of failing to treat the extravaganza with the seriousness it deserved:

> The UK has double standards in the Contest. It is something you love to hate. It's something to laugh at. It's something continental. It's a scam. It's ridiculous. The British like to distance themselves from it.

Bjørn Erichsen, right, with Misa Molk, a Slovenian member of the Reference Group, the day her term ended, June 2008. Erichsen retired in January 2010.

Erichsen perhaps was remembering Wogan's description of the ESC in Copenhagen, a show the Dane was very proud of, where the BBC commentator kept mocking the presenters, Natasja Crone Back and Søren Pilmark, referring to them as 'Dr. Death and the Tooth Fairy'.

Erichsen always stuck to his guns about the Eurovision's image: 'Terry Wogan is a problem because he makes it ridiculous.' He invited Sir Terry to address the EBU's annual gathering in Lucerne, called Eurovision TV, in May 2009, in the run-up to the Moscow Contest, Graham Norton's first. The Dane even took on the veteran broadcaster in good-humored debate for the delegates.

Jørgen Franck, another Danish national, but with a different, less abrasive management style, who'd been Ericsen's deputy, succeeded him in 2010, before departing after an EBU shake-up two years later. His career trajectory was interesting, as he had spent two decades as a classical musician, playing the principal oboe in the Danish Radio Sinfonietta, before he took advantage of his Master's degree in Law to occupy the post of Head of Legal Affairs at Danish broadcaster DR, and began a career in Geneva from there.

Franck, in his convivial style, summed up the Contest in 2011, saying that the music is a tool to bring the people and the broadcasters of Europe together:

> To me, the song contest is a battlefield where you can allow yourself to be a patriot. You can even allow yourself to be a nationalist, which is a word you don't want to attach much to people these days. You can support your own country. You can say the others stink. It's harmless but it's very significant. If we didn't have that battlefield, we might have more battles.[10]

To what extent the EBU and their executive supervisor intervene in the preparations for each Eurovision is a diplomatic issue. The individ-

---

[10] *Quoted in:* Performing the 'New' Europe, *edited by Karen Fricker and Milija Gluhovic, Palgrave MacMillan, 2013.*

ual broadcaster, and government in some cases, comes up with most of the cost, so they like to use the Eurovision to 'express themselves'. Some countries find the formula a little restricting. The event manager for the Oslo Contest in 2010, Stina Greaker, describes the production and organization of the ESC as somewhat 'liturgical', meaning that too much is, in a way, laid down.

> I think in principle it is strange that the host broadcaster – who is mostly paying for the entire event and the TV broadcast, decides so little!

Stockselius thinks that there was enough free rein to host countries in his time in charge:

> I often said that I want it to look different should we be in Istanbul, Moscow or Paris. Unlike the MTV Awards as an example, where the same crew produce the show to look exactly the same with no local flavor at all.'

In Stina Greaker's experience, it's a little different. She describes the agreement the host broadcaster, in her case NRK, must sign with the EBU as 'quite entertaining', with riders about the number of cars with a driver, and how many ornamental trees there must be in the different offices the EBU will use at the event. She says also that the EBU's marketing partners, TEAM, who take care of the sponsors and the city branding, had, in her experience:

> ... a somewhat patronizing attitude towards the organizers. It was actually quite funny, but also annoying at times.

A big test came for Stockselius early in the job. Ukraine had won the 2004 Contest in Istanbul with Ruslana and *Wild Dances*. NTU was the country's national broadcaster so they were due to host the event in 2005. But then all hell broke loose in the country, in what turned out to be only the first of the upheavals, known as the 'Orange Revolution'. They had a song contest to organise, but the country – and the broadcaster – was in turmoil. It was touch and go that spring as to whether

Stina Greaker, event manager for Oslo in 2010. The recent practice is to have an overall executive producer (in Oslo it was Jon Ola Sand who later succeeded Svante Stockselius as ESC Executive Supervisor) and another to take charge of logistics to do with the event, including the transport and accommodation.

there'd be a Eurovision that year. A substitute city was even discussed. Stockselius describes the events of that spring as 'probably the most serious crisis in the history of the Contest'.

In February, three months before the event, he was informed there were no hotels booked, no venue hired, no one in charge for important areas of this huge project. The new political leadership of the country had fired all the previous ones. So Stockselius started to investigate the drastic prospect of moving the Contest to another country. Then he was asked whether he could come along to an important meeting. He was taken to the President's office where the newly installed leader, Mr. Yushchenko, was waiting with a group of his ministers and the Mayor of Kiev. Svante recalls the conversation:

The president started by saying, 'I believe we have some problems.' I answered: 'Yes, you do Mr. President.' I went through the nineteen most important issues that were not solved and the president handed over each problem to one of the ministers present. He asked me to come back in two weeks. I did, to the same room and the same serious faces. Mr. President opened the meeting: 'Mr. Stockselius, I am sorry but I must make you disappointed…' At that moment I saw the Contest moving somewhere else. Then he smiled and said, 'We have only solved 18 of the 19 matters, the last one will be solved tomorrow…' And they sure did, in less than three months we managed to get everything in place.

The crisis brought an opportunity for one young man. The room with the president had a few older men in it, and one twenty-something-year-old. His name was Pavlo Grytsak, and he had been one of the people behind the Ruslana victory. So Yushchenko dispensed with seniority and made him Ukraine's boss for the Contest.

Jill Paulsson worked as Svante's assistant at that time. She believes that the ESC is clearly not only about entertainment, but about politics and human rights too:

Experiencing the Orange Revolution first hand in Kiev that year made a big impression on me. The people wanted so much to get closer to Europe that time. Sad to see that they are still fighting so hard.

Yushchenko is now largely forgotten, and Ukraine's upheaval didn't end there, sadly. There's unintended forboding of that country's current difficulties in the description in Tim Moore's *Nul Points* of a protest outside the stadium that year by pro-Russians, objecting to the country's entry that year, Green Jolly, and their song, *Together We Are Many*. One banner read, 'Europe – Green Jolly is not Ukraine!'

At a seminar in Amsterdam in 2006, Stockselius brought a radical idea up for discussion, wondering whether more 'jeopardy' was needed in the Contest. Reality shows were sweeping television sched-

The Reference Group Chairperson for many years, Ruurd Bierman from The Netherlands. Frank-Dieter Freiling from Germany succeeded him in 2009.

ules across Europe. The idea for Eurovision was that instead of announcing the semi-final qualifiers on the night of the semi (this was still in the one semi-final era), all the delegations would instead be brought to the green room on the night of the final. The artists would be in their stage costumes and made up and they would be called – or not called – to the stage. Interesting, but cruel, was the consensus. The idea was floated again informally in the following years. In the end, it was felt that the Eurovision was doing just fine and was neither 'broke' nor needing 'fixing'.

Stockselius worked closely with the chairman of the Reference Group, the commanding Dutchman Ruurd Bierman, also chairman of the EBU's Television Committee. A charismatic, 'Peter Pan-like' figure, he descibed himself on his own website as '**one of Europe's thought leaders on the future of media**'.

Both men were skilled at handling diplomatic issues. There was one such problem in Serbia in the run up to the Belgrade Contest. The Reference Group was presented with the image designs for the Contest that BRT, the Serbian broadcaster, had commissioned. They were particularly poor, it was agreed. A difficult discussion ensued where Bierman and Stockselius tactically allowed others in the group to make the running, keeping a diplomatic silence. Lunch brought a break and as we looked out over the partially frozen Danube, one of us had a brainwave. 'You've got two rivers meeting here in Belgrade, could there be a concept in that?'

So 'Confluence of Sound' was born. Viewers will remember the final, classy graphic where 'tins of blue and red paint', Serbian colours, representing the Danube and Sava rivers, were 'thrown' at each other and merged.

There were bigger questions that surfaced on Svante's watch. There was some support in the Reference Group to change the rules to both allow more artists on the stage, and to allow vocals on the backing track. A Swedish member, Christer Björkman, who represented Sweden as a singer in 1992 and went on to be one of the central figures in Melodifestivalen, drove the proposal. His point was, 'Look

The 'Confluence of Sound' graphic for the Serbian Contest

how polished the Swedish final had become. Look at *X Factor* – does anybody notice when backing vocals aren't live?' Despite his own Melodifestivalen past, the Executive Supervisor was sceptical. The discussion lingered on until after the Svante era, before being buried.

Protecting the Contest's image was something Stockselius, Bierman and the Reference Group were always focused on. Stockselius looks back favourably now on the 'Finnish monsters' intervention in 2006, but not so at Ireland's two years later:

> I think Lordi well deserved the win. They had a great song, an exciting stage act and modernized the Contest for sure. I was a lot more worried of the Irish entry with the puppet. That caused a true image problem, one of the participating

countries clearly stated that 'we do not take this seriously'. I was ashamed by this.

Towards the end of 2009, Stockselius was saying to colleagues that he didn't intend to remain in the job forever. He knew that his safe guiding of the Contest through a crucial phase of its history was acknowledged. There was a personal factor too. He had become a father rather late in life – in his early fifties – and the travelling schedule in the job was interfering with this.

But Svante's future was really decided by a shake-up in the EBU. A new Director General, Ingrid Deltenre, took up her position in January 2010. Change was her platform. She's a Dutch and Swiss national, and had been CEO of Schweizer Fernsehen (SF), the leading public TV broadcaster in the German-speaking region of Switzerland. The Eurovision Song Contest, the 'jewel of the EBU' was to be run in future from

Candid moment: Svante Stockselius (right), with Ruurd Bierman (centre), Chairman of the Reference Group, and Bjørn Ericson (left), the EBU's Television Director, during the Reference Group's de-briefing meeting in Stockholm in June 2009, following the Moscow Contest. The Svante years were coming to an end.

Representatives of the participating countries and members of the NRK team at the Heads of Delegation meeting in Oslo in March 2010, in front of the city's famous Opera House. Stockselius is back row, eighth from the right. On his right is the man who became his successor as Executive Supervisor of the Contest, Jon Ola Sand.

EBU Headquarters in Geneva, not, as it had been quite successfully, from Stockholm. Neither Svante nor Kati Varblane, his assistant who was based in Talinn, were prepared to move to the Swiss city. There was a certain amount of 'bluff calling' on both sides, but in the end the Stockselius era was over.

The EBU then advertised the 'most important job in European television entertainment'. After a process that included interviews, the selection board turned their attention to a TV executive in Norway, the man who had very effectively managed the Oslo Contest the previous year but hadn't applied for the job, Jon Ola Sand, and 'head-hunted' him. The competent and personable Sand, has been in the job since. A Dutchman, Sietse Bakker, who founded the esctoday.com website when he was sixteen, and who takes charge of press and the Eurovision event, as well as the Junior Eurovision Song Contest, is second in command.

Stockselius once joked modestly about how uneasy he felt when passing a picture of himself at Stockholm's Arlanda airport, part of a series featuring Swedish achievers in the world. He reflects on his ESC time:

> I don't miss it. I like to live in the present and not in the past. I really enjoyed my eight years of running this great show – but that was then. Now I watch it from my favorite TV-chair. I didn't leave it even when the Contest was being held in Sweden in 2013.'

Stockselius and his Reference Group colleagues had, in 2008, seen through what turned out to be a public relations triumph for the Contest – the limited return of juries.

Bledar Sejko, who along with Adrian Lulgjuraj, represented Albania in the Contest in Malmö in 2013. (Photo: Albin Olsson)

Chapter 10

'Bring Back the Juries!'

'Who knows what hellish future lies ahead?' said Terry Wogan, introducing the Helsinki Contest in 2007 to his BBC viewers, before adding: 'Actually, I do. I've seen the rehearsals.' Terry might be flattered to know that, by his commentary in general, he had an inadvertent role in a rule change that was brewing for the Contest.

The American academic and ESC aficionado, Karen Fricker, considered the Wogan phenomenon in 2012 in an essay entitled, 'Terry Wogan, Melancholy Britain, and the Eurovision Song Contest':

> When UK media figures, including Wogan, trash-talk Eurovision, I contend, they are addressing feelings of un-processed anger, frustration, and loss about the country's changing relationship to Europe and the rest of the world.

Fricker knows of course that, to his credit, Wogan had made a lot of people laugh over the years, so she turns to analyse humour's role in all this:

> The function of Wogan's humour, in my view, is not to gird viewers against inevitable embarrassment but rather unite them by pointing out aspects of the Contest that are inscrutable or seemingly absurd, and offering readings of those aspects, thereby constructing a discursive community that

understands itself as perhaps a part of, but certainly different from, the rest of Europe.[11]

As it happened, that spring of 2009 when Wogan announced his retirement from his 38-year-long commentator role, the Reference Group and the EBU in Geneva had already agreed a change to the voting procedure, re-introducing the juries' role in deciding the winner, after eleven years. There is a view that the motivation for the decision was the EBU trying to help, or satisfy the 'Big Four' countries (as they were then, having since become the 'Big Five' after Italy's return). This is not the case.

There were long discussions in the Reference Group in the second half of 2008. Debate centred around three issues: the evidence that diasporas were influencing the vote; the negative effect this had on the image of the Song Contest; and the fact that Eurovision hadn't produced a hit record for a long time which was an issue for its credibility – and its capacity to draw bigger stars, particularly in the West.

Against this was the contrary argument: why should five people in a room have the same voting power as the entire population of each country, and to take the example of Russia, it means five versus 140 million? Wasn't the televote more democratic? There was also a fear that the televote and its revenue would decline. But the diaspora issue was the major argument in favour of change.

The term 'diaspora voting' was coined by the esctoday.com website in 2006. To look at the phenomenon and its influence on the Contest requires some number crunching. It also involves a glimpse at the 'ethno history' of Europe.

First, let's take the example of Estonia, a Baltic republic that's now an EU member, but for many years was part of the Soviet Union. The four largest non-Estonian ethic groups in the country are: Russians, 25 per cent; Ukrainians, 2.1 per cent; Belarusians, 1.2 per cent; Finns, 0.8 per cent. In the 2007 Contest the Estonian televote awarded points as

---

[11] Quoted in: *Performing the 'New' Europe,* edited by Karen Fricker and Milija Gluhovic, Palgrave MacMillan, 2013.

follows: Russia, twelve points; Latvia, ten points; Ukraine eight points; Finland seven points. Was it musical taste, or emotion, or a bit of neigh-bourliness? We'll never know, but the correlation is clear.

Next, the southwest of Europe: Spain's top three countries from its televote result in 2007 were Romania, twelve points; Bulgaria, ten points and Armenia eight points. Fascinatingly, the largest ethnic mi-norities in Spain are: Romanian, 9.2 per cent; Bulgarian, 4.45 per cent, Ukraine, 2.69 per cent and Armenian, 2.1 per cent. So a definite correla-tion, it would appear. Next, the example of Germany. In the 2007 final, the 'German people' awarded twelve points to Turkey; ten points to Greece and eight to Serbia. Turkish people are the largest minority in Germany, followed by Italy (not participating in the ESC in 2007), then Serbian and Greek immigrants.

In Ireland, the figures were only a little less dramatic. The minori-ties in Ireland are in the following order by population: British, Poles, Americans, Lithuanians, Latvians, Germans and Russians. Televot-ers in Ireland that year, 2007, awarded points as follows: Lithuania, twelve; Latvia, ten, United Kingdom, seven; Russia, six. (Poland had received ten points from Ireland in the semi-final, but hadn't qualified). Incidentally, Irish viewers gave their eight to Serbia, which, though it doesn't have a significant diaspora in Ireland, was the winning song.

Why would such relatively small numbers of people apparently have such a disproportionate influence on the voting? Motivation is one reason; the Eurovision gives emigrants a chance to show solidarity with their home place. The general audience only has their own taste as a motivation. As well as this, only about one in twenty viewers of Eurovision actually take part in the televote; in political election par-lance, it's a 'low poll'.

Jørgen Franck of the EBU, referring in 2012 to return of juries, put it this way:

We said, 'Ok, let's have a test of the public vote by an expert vote of an expert jury. Let's see if it actually changes the result?' We had a suspicion it wouldn't change much.'[12]

And it didn't change very much. The following table shows the top ten places in the split jury/televote result for the first Contest decided by 50/50 voting, Moscow in 2009.

Eurovision Song Contest Final 2009				
Place	**Televoting**	**Points**	**Jury**	**Points Result (Combined)**
1	Norway	378	Norway	312 **Norway**
2	Azerbaijan	253	Iceland	260 **Iceland**
3	Turkey	203	UK	223 **Azerbaijan**
4	Iceland	173	France	164 **Turkey**
5	Greece	151	Estonia	124 **UK**
6	Estonia	129	Denmark	120 **Estonia**
7	Bosnia and Herzegovina	124	Turkey	114 **Greece**
8	Russia	118	Azerbaijan	112 **France**
9	Armenia	111	Israel	107 **Bosnia and Herzegovina**
10	UK	105	Moldova	93 **Armenia**

First place was exactly the same, with Norway winning by a large margin in both polls. Seven countries that featured in the top ten in

---

[12] Quoted in: *Performing the 'New' Europe,* edited by Karen Fricker and Milija Gluhovic, Palgrave MacMillan, 2013

both the televote and jury vote also featured in the combined result, albeit in a different position. For example, Azerbaijan was second in the televote, eighth in the jury vote, and third in the combined result – the official Eurovision result.

A small difference came in terms of East–West balance, 'old' Europe taking the top four places with the juries and, in the top ten places, five were from this part of the continent as chosen by the televote, seven with the jury vote.

The most commented-on result from the juries was the fact that two of the 'Big Four' had their best result for a number of years: France came eighth (fourth with the juries) and the UK, fifth (third with the juries). It appeared that the fortunes of these countries – in the voting – had changed, or had it? France had sent a big star, with a profile in many parts of Europe, Patricia Kaas. The UK had Andrew Lloyd Webber on board. The following year in Oslo, the United Kingdom were twenty-fifth – last – in both the jury, the televote and, consequently, the overall result. France came twelfth, having come eighteenth with the jury vote and, ironically, eighth in the televote.

However, in 2011 the Eurovision winner would have been Raphael Gualazzi with the jazzy number, *Madness of Love* for Italy had the juries alone made the decision. Italy, the ESC veteran participant nearly pulled off a big coup on their return to the Contest. But they had to settle for second place; coming eleventh place in the televote brought their combined vote down.

The 'split vote' information is not revealed by the EBU until the publicity for the winner has died down, and even then it's low key. The fear is that if 'all three' results were known on the night of the final, there's the possibility of having 'three winners'. So it was agreed by the Reference Group that this information should be 'managed' as it were.

The results in 2013 and 2014 are further proof there's no 'smoking gun' in the Eurovision voting system. As one fan remarked to me in 2012: 'Jury members are punters too!' Below is a table from 2014 showing, except for Poland, the same five countries in the top five in the three votes.

Place	Televoting	Points	Jury	Points Official Result
1	Austria	311	Austria	224 Austria
2	Netherlands	222	Sweden	201 Netherlands
3	Armenia	193	Netherlands	200 Sweden
4	Sweden	190	Hungary	138 Armenia
5	Poland	162	Armenia	125 Hungary

There was another tweak in 2013. Instead of each national jury ranking the other competing countries on a one to ten basis, they would now continue and rank all, down to their last preference, a full ranking in other words. It was considered fairer by the EBU. It means that it is possible for a country that scored highly in the televote or the jury vote not making it into the points awarded (the one to seven and the eight, ten and twelve) at all because of scoring really low in the other ranking.

On a less complicated note, having juries in each country has encouraged a harmless little sport among Eurovision delegations: Heads of Delegation can generally find out after the second dress rehearsal on the Friday before the final (the 'Jury Final' as it's called) how their national jury voted. They can then 'trade the information' with other countries' delegations, and maybe get a sense of the fate that awaits them when all the votes are in.

This chapter began with Terry Wogan, so it ends with him. He 'came back', in a manner of speaking, to comment on Conchita Wurst's win. Reviewing Graham Norton's book *The Life and Loves of a He-Devil* in *The Irish Times*, he endorsed his successor Norton – but with a sting:

> He made it his own from year one – although I'm bound to say that the Bearded Lady who won this year, reducing Graham to tears, might have had a slightly different effect on me. I've always seen the Eurovision as a sometimes foolish farce, but not as a freak show.

Kasey Smith onstage for Ireland in Copenhagen in 2014. The act's look was criticised as 'Celtic kitch'. The song, Heartbeat, *failed to qualify from the semi-final. (Photo: Albin Olsson)*

A winner returns: Niamh Kavanagh, who won the contest in 1993, 'goes native' in the Arctic Circle in 2010. The airline, Norwegian, a sponsor that year, organized a trip to the Samiland region during the Oslo Contest. Niamh was representing Ireland for a second time, qualifying for the final and finishing twenty-third. Interestingly the song, It's For You, picked up sixty-seven points in the semi-final, joint ninth out of seventeen countries, but only managed a score of twenty-five at the final with thirty-eight countries voting.

Chapter 11

Vienna and Beyond

It's curiously appropriate – or inappropriate, perhaps, to some – that the Eurovision celebrates its sixtieth Contest in that great home of music, Vienna. On streets walked by Mozart, Beethoven and Haydn, to name just three, the fans, the press and the singers will gather in May. In the city's famous coffee shops, with their soft chairs and elegant marble tables, the talk will be of various countries' singers, dancers, costumes – and their chances.

As they present the city, the organisers will exploit its great connection with the golden age of classical music. The Director General of ORF (Österreichischer Rundfunk), Alexander Wrabetz, told Eurovision.tv when the host city was announced:

> Vienna is the city of music and arts in the heart of Europe. Together we will do everything to assure a successful 60th Eurovision Song Contest.

More than 150 years before backing tracks and pop music were heard of, Josef Haydn, the doyen of the Vienna Classic period of the late eighteenth century, was able to say 'My language is spoken throughout the world'. What would he, or his great admirer Mozart, have made of their fellow Austrian, Thomas Neuwirth, known to the world since 2014 as Conchita Wurst? Wolfgang Amadeus certainly had colourful and vigorous characters in his operas. So could there be a connection between Conchita and the 'Queen of the Night' from *The Magic Flute*?

The Contest's 2014 winner, Conchita Wurst, onstage in Copenhagen
(Photo: Albin Olsson)

The Queen of the Night's aria, *Der Hölle Rache Kocht in Meinem Herzen,* is one of the most well known of opera arias, demanding a two octave range from the soprano. It begins:

> The vengeance of Hell boils in my heart
> Death and despair flame about me!

With Wurst presenting in Vienna, and the LGBT activists getting worked up, the sixtieth Eurovision is sure to produce its share of surprises, controversies, songs that sound like others, and moments of magic. Then, by midnight on 23 May, as another artist celebrates their achievement and wonders what it will bring them, the lights will have gone off for another year and the crews will be stripping the stage.

There will be singers with glorious moments, others with bad hair days and costume horrors, and academics who will look at things like 'human rights and sexuality discourse', or 'conundrums of post-socialist belonging' in the Eurovision Song Contest; others who will say they liked a particular song, but not the singer's make up, and the majority who will sip their drinks and enjoy the fun.

As for its future, some might say the growing homogenisation of popular music may threaten musical diversity, but Aileen Dillane of the Irish World Academy of Music and Dance doesn't agree:

> I think that has been proven over and over again not to be the case, and with growing migration across and into Europe, I think the musical landscape will be enriched, not diminished.

She believes you can't ignore the power nostalgia has for us all:

> I remember sitting on the edge of my grandmother's stairs, sneaking out of bed to catch a peak of the Irish entry which was on late in the evening. Now I make an event of it for my children. So as long as the national networks and the EBU continues, so too will the Eurovision.

Niamh Kavanagh concurs:

It was time we spent as a family, choosing our favourites and supporting Ireland. I was twelve when Johnny won first and it was amazing to me that Ireland could win at such a big event.

Perhaps the Eurovision Song Contest will last as long as men and women can sit down, at a piano or with a guitar, and write songs that connect with other people's sadness, joy and dreams. That should be a while yet.

Niamh Kavanagh singing It's For You *in Oslo, May 2010*

Index